THE SECRET HERDS
Animal Stories

Also available in the Target series:

THE SECRET HERDS

Animal Stories

JOYCE STRANGER

Illustrated by Douglas Reay

First published in Great Britain by
J. M. Dent & Sons, Ltd, 1974
First published in this edition by
Tandem Publishing Ltd, 1976

ISBN 0 426 11017 X

*These stories are all fiction. No event happened;
no character ever existed.*

Dedicated to Tom Henry
of the *Manchester Evening News*,
who first published the germ of these stories
in his paper.

Target Books are published by Tandem Publishing Ltd,
14 Gloucester Road, London SW7 4RD.
A Howard & Wyndham Company

Printed in Great Britain by Richard Clay
(The Chaucer Press) Ltd, Bungay, Suffolk

CONTENTS

Snow on Low Ground

He was very small.

He was very lonely.

He was very hungry.

His name was Shala. He was a dog otter, born that year in a deep holt in the steep bank of the Rushing River. His birth bed was lined with leaves, dead and dry, that rustled when he moved. The first sounds he knew were the crackle of bedding, and the racing surge of the water that swept past the opening under the willow tree. It was many days before he saw what caused the noise.

When high summer came and the river was green-edged with wild flowers and rushes, he and his two sisters learned to swim and to follow their mother down the slippery bank and land with a wild flurry of sheer delight in the glittery water. Here he caught his first fish. Here was home.

He was too young at first to be aware of change. But change came swiftly, so that he was half grown, and then full grown, and his sisters left home to pair with other dog otters, and his mother found her mate, an old dog who would not have his son about him. He chased Shala away with snap of teeth and vicious snarl, and a sharp nip in the flank when the younger otter stared, disbelieving, wanting company.

The old dog bit again, and Shala fled, stopping only

when he was a mile away to paw at his smarting nose, and to stare forlornly at a sky that had forgotten warmth, and to curl alone in a bracken clump while the first frost cut the air with vicious teeth. The little otter sniffed the strangeness and wondered what was coming. He had no experience or memory to guide him. Only the instinct that taught all wild beasts, and the need for food and survival.

He watched the red fox run through the woods, a cock pheasant dangling from his jaws. He listened to the jays' angry scream, as the hunter passed. He learned that sometimes the fox did not eat all his kill and, when fishing was bad and hunger his master, he thieved from outside the den when the fox lay curled, nosetip to tailtip, deep underground, dreaming of plump young rabbits.

Food was scarce for all. There were so many beasts running, and owl, fox, badger and otter foraged and fed sparely. Chemicals ran into the river, the fish were few and the water tasted bad. They drank from the rain pools that lay in the grey rocks that pushed out of the earth, and they ate when they could.

Shala found a new holt under the rushes and slept safe and warm until rain from the hills filled the Rushing River, which left its bed and poured over the fields so that his home was under water. The river tore away the banks, and when it went down there was desolation and a smell that drove Shala to look for another resting place.

The year had forgotten warmth. The days were icy cold, the skies dismal, the clouds wind-driven, packing in grey masses that fled across the blue, hiding it, Shala felt, for

ever. Summer was a dim memory. Each day was a bitter test. The icy wind from the north stroked his fur, stung his eyes and chilled his paws. He crouched and huddled inside his holt, but life was all discomfort and, to add to his misery, rain often poured from a steely sky.

He loved the river, but he did not like rain. He liked to sleep dry, and that was becoming impossible. He liked to feed well, and that too was not possible. And each day he knew he was more lonely.

Sometimes he clambered up a little hill and lifted his nose to the sky and whistled, the sound sweet and soft and filled with longing. Nothing answered him. He was loneliest of all at night, when the yellow moon hung, a glowing ball, in the dark that crept over the horizon, and the plaint of owls swung into the air, echo answering echo, so that once more he whistled and listened, but heard only the soulless repeat of the sound from the close-packed woods.

Every night was frosty now. Bare trees were etched against the midnight sky. The moon was clear and the earth grew harder with each passing hour, the grass was grey-glittering with frost, the trees were leafless, and the fallen leaves under his paws were scarred and crisp and cold.

He left the woods and followed the river, which surged wide and dark and full, carrying floating branches and debris from the floods on its swelling surface. Here there was enough water to dilute the chemicals and here once more were fish. He fed again, but the fish were cunning and hard to catch and he did not feed well.

One night he came for the first time to a human home. He stopped outside the gate, and stared at the dark bulk of the house, at the mysterious moon likeness caught inside it, at the shadows that crossed the windows.

The door opened, spilling light across his path, and he shrank into the bushes as a giant creature on two legs, with strange-looking fur, came into the garden and called aloud,

'Puss, puss, where are you then? Puss, puss?'

Nothing moved, and after a few more minutes' calling the door was shut and the creature went inside. The otter nosed his way forward, among the dead stiff stalks of the Michaelmas daisies, smelling fish, which the woman was cooking for the cat's supper. Shala knew nothing about

cats, and never yet, in all his small life, had he been threatened by any living creature except the big dog otter. He crept forward again.

The cat was an old and striped tom, a warrior of many years and the winner of many memorable battles. His tiger fur was dark streaked on ginger, his head proud, his one ear torn and tattered, the other almost gone. He smelled otter, and he froze in the darkness, his green eyes glittering greedily. He forgot the rat beneath his paws. That was dead. This creature beyond him was alive and warm, and the need to kill was a need he could never deny. His long, barred tail swayed to and fro, dreamily at first, and then faster.

The otter moved towards the house, attracted by the

tantalizing smell that made his mouth water, and his tongue lick his lips, and his belly cry out with hunger. He moved slowly, cautiously, but he did not scent the cat. The wind betrayed Shala and hid Tom.

The tabby tiger sprang.

Shala rolled, flash-lightning fast. His heavy tail caught Tom across the face, but old Tom had fought many battles. He twisted, eel-like, and slashed with raking claws. The furious paw caught Shala's shoulder and did no harm. His fur was very thick. He twisted in his turn and tried to bite. His teeth glanced off Tom's leg, and Tom squealed his fury.

The otter snarled.

The front door opened, spilling light.

'Tom, you varmint. What are you doing?' a voice asked, and water spilled in a soaking flood across cat and otter. Tom withdrew and shook himself and the two-legged creature bent and picked him up.

'You don't fight otters. Let the poor beast run, and come you in, you rascal,' the voice went on. The words washed over Shala's head, meaningless.

He watched the woman carry the cat indoors and shut the light in with her. He shook his wet coat. Water meant little to him, but this night was freezing hard and star-shine bright, the ice so fierce it almost glittered in the air, the trees unfamiliar, hoarfrost clad, and the grass needle sharp and Christmas glorious, the moon dazzling on the ground. Ice cracked on his fur within minutes of the dowsing.

Shala ran. He was thirsty and he was still hungry, and behind him the smell of cooking fish hung on the air tantalizingly. His mouth was sore with the saliva that flooded at every step. His mind had only one thought. Food! Food! Food! Food was more necessary hourly. He was so hungry that he was weak. His footsteps dragged. Beyond him lay the river. He ran down the bank.

He dived.

Minutes later he picked himself up, dazed. Ice covered the water. The river was frozen solid. Shala could not believe it. He struck at the hard surface with nose and paw, and then ran, whimpering, so hungry he did not know where he was going. He could not reach the fish. He could not understand where the water had gone. He walked on the ice, and his paws slipped and he slid, unable to balance. He snarled, but there was no enemy to fight. He was helpless.

At last he reached the bank. He climbed up and found himself a hollow in a tree trunk, sheltered from the wind. He curled up, nose to tail, and slept, but he did not sleep well. He was so empty that the cold was chilling him, and he was dimly aware, through instincts ages old, that he must seek food. Any food.

The hunting owl was hungry too. The running fox was half-starved. Stoat and weasel all hankered for food. On the hill the deer pawed the hard ground, eating frozen moss. The little birds shivered and died on the branches. The berries were gone.

That night the wind changed. The icy chill vanished and a warm airstream covered the land. When Shala woke, everything he knew had disappeared. The trees were covered in white. The ground was smoothed and softened, and glittered in the early sun. The ice on the river was hidden. The little otter had never seen snow before.

He pawed it, anxious, afraid that it might bite. Nothing happened. He licked it, and it melted in his mouth, and he knew at once that this was water, this was a soothing for the thirst that parched him. He ate the snow, holding it in his mouth till it was warm inside him. It revived him, and he ventured out and stared about him.

Behind him, even the cottage where he had fought the cat was deep in snow. Only its chimney showed, hard red against the white, a foam of smoke pluming from the stack, bulking into the air, a tiny cloud above the human home.

Beyond him there were no bushes, no heather, no grass. He walked cautiously, his paws sinking deep, his tail dragging behind him, so that later the keeper saw the tracks and knew that an otter had been that way.

He came to a small clearing. Here was food. Food put down for the birds and the deer, and the birds were feeding. They saw Shala and, chattering angrily, flew to the nearby trees. He did not notice the little hut where the workmen sheltered. It too was white. One of them had thrown down seed and bread, sorry for the starving creatures. The men were building a pipeline through the woods. There were three loaves broken into large rough pieces. Shala had never tasted bread before. He approached cautiously, sniffing suspiciously. It smelled of man. It smelled of something else strange too, that he did not understand. The man smoked an old pipe and the bread was fouled with tobacco.

Shala was too hungry to care. He took the largest hunk

he could find, almost half a loaf, and ran with it, back to the hollow tree, where he was hidden from all eyes. He ate every scrap and his busy tongue licked up the crumbs and this time he slept, his aching emptiness eased.

Snow fell all day, large silent flakes that masked the world anew and banked up deep against the hollow in the tree. Shala was trapped, but the bread had saved his life and he slept until the thaw came three days later, and the mysterious cover began to turn to slush.

Once more it froze.

Once more he found mysterious offerings in the wood. This time the men had pitied the wildlings and had flung more than bread. Shala found the leg of a cooked chicken, before the fox came hunting, and tasted cooked meat. He preferred fish, but the food helped him survive, and for three weeks he scavenged with the birds, feeding on man's bounty, while the river lay in icy thrall, snow fell, melted, and fell again. In man's world Christmas came and went, and the first chill January days brought more discomfort to the beasts that lived in the wild.

The men could not work, but the old man came daily. He sometimes hid himself among the trees and watched the beasts that fed. He was proud of the otter, but told no one, for they hunted in those parts and, when summer came, might extract the price of his skin from the little beast. He was small, the man noted, and young, but his head was beautiful, and when he looked towards the trees the brown eyes were doglike, reminding the man of the many dogs he had owned in a life that was now reaching towards almost a century. Ninety-two years old, and he looked forward to spending his hundredth birthday still caring for the beasts he loved. Eight years was not a long time for an old man. The days flicked past, ever faster, so that where once they had stretched endless, now there was barely time to do the jobs that needed doing between dawn and dark. His grandson worked on the pipeline and the old man brought him food daily, and his grandson's friends teased him, telling him what a hale old boy he was, and asking what creatures he had seen, knowing how well he knew the wild.

He would not tell them of the otter.

Thaw freed the river from its pall of ice. Shala dived deep, revelling in the water, caught three fish in quick succession and fed gluttonously, filling himself with food. He was soon restored. The sun shone, a weak January sun, but behind it was a small promise of warmth to come, and the little otter left the river and hunted through the woods, sniffing at new scents that the snow had freed. He knew the weasel had come that way, and that the deer had been foraging. He visited the food pile and took a hunk of bread back to his hollow tree, but he did not eat it. It was provision against another time of hunger.

That night was the first night that he was free from the need to hunt food. When the moon hung low over the trees, a giant glowing ball, he explored the ground. In one place he found a steep slope, still snow-covered, facing the north wind, where warmth never penetrated until summer was more than a rumour on the air.

He slipped and skidded down the slope, tobogganing. Faster and faster, speeding towards the bottom, to land with a thud on the soft deep drift that still filled the hollow. He dug himself out and shook, suddenly merry, wanting to play, at ease and happy.

He climbed the hill.

He flew down again, this time on purpose, enjoying the swift flight, the impression of wings, free as the birds in the air, as they slid down the warm airstreams, gliding. Again and again he plunged, from top to bottom, until there was an icy slide that gave him even more speed. He dived and climbed, dived and climbed, in an ecstasy of achievement, and forgot the world that could be cruel, knowing only delight. He was still sliding when the sun ran over the horizon.

He returned to the river, and fished and fed, but now another need was mastering him. He had to explore. He whistled, wanting company, wanting another otter to play with, wanting a warm body curled close against his side, a warm tongue to lick him, warm fur that he could lick himself. The urge was stronger than hunger. There was a scent, faint on the air, that summoned him.

He whistled again, sweet and shrill and clear.

Only the birdcalls answered him.

He turned to the west and ran on.

He ran over a moor, where snow still lay in the hollows, among the dry, dead heather and the rusty bracken that caught the gold from the sun.

He crossed a road and dived deep into a ditch, and lay shaking. A vast monster roared towards him, headlights flashing, as the lorry breasted the hill.

When all was quiet again and darkness reassured him, he clambered out of the ditch. There was a distant orange glow in the sky. He saw it, but it meant nothing. He turned away from the lights that flared from the town, and crossed a garden, unseen, leaving tracks in the flower bed that baffled the children next day. He came into a street, smelling of man, and hurried down it, hunting for sanctuary, and very afraid. A dog barked, smelling the otter, and an angry voice silenced it, unable to see anything outside to cause alarm. The dog settled, nose on paws, disconsolate and misunderstood. He had only been doing his duty and he did not know the beast outside was harmless to his family.

There was an odd noise in the night, a roaring angry surge. The otter turned again, down a narrow lane, between high hedges, towards a powerful fishy smell that told him here was food. He came out of the lane and stared. There was more water than he had ever seen in his life. It was angry water, flinging itself against the rocks, spraying skyward in a shock of foam, flying high against the moon. The waves crashed in rolling thunder on the shingle.

Shala ran along the beach and played with the smaller waves, but he was wary of the wild ones that came surging, white-fanged, towards him. He discovered a rock pool. Here were three fish stranded by the tide. He took them and ate them. He had already learned. He ran along the sea-shore, searching the rocks, finding shellfish as well as seafish. There was food here, in plenty.

He returned to the narrow lane, hiding himself inside a rabbit hole under the bank beneath the hedge. It had been deserted long ago, and was warm and dry and sandy.

The wind dropped. The tide turned, and in the early dawn, when men were still in bed and few beasts were about, Shala woke, stretched himself, scratched and ran down to the sea again, where he found new cause for wondering.

Where last night had been only angry water, was now salt sand, a golden stretch which took his pawmarks and showed where he had tracked. He ran down to the water's edge. Tiny waves brushed the sandbank. A seagull soared above him. A tern flew low over the beach towards the water and Shala chased it in fun, not hunting, only wanting to speed after this creature that tore through the air with such effortless speed. The tern banked and soared, and then Shala was in the water, swimming away from the shore.

He rolled and dived and surfaced and lay on his back, basking in the sunshine that held a hint of warmth in its rays. The birds dived to look at him, and dived for fish, so that splashes sounded all around him. He floated, blissful. The cold water could not penetrate his underfur. It was too thick and well waterproofed, and protected him from ice.

He landed on a deserted beach, and ran into the wood beyond the grass that bordered the sand. He lifted his head. There was that scent on the air again, sweet and enticing, exciting and attracting. It woke new needs inside him. He followed it, sometimes catching it, nose-high, airborne, sometimes searching for it on the ground. He forgot food. He forgot daylight and danger, and tracked on.

At the top of a tiny hill he stopped and whistled. There was birdnoise, there was a dog barking, there was the sound of the sea, now only a gentle murmur. Somewhere a train sang, two quick notes, that drowned a small echo of Shala's cry. He whistled again, sure there must be an answer.

Far away, came a soft thin call that sent him skeltering down the hill, through the wood, so that the birds cried after him, unaware that he held no threat. The smell was stronger, was a catch in his throat, was a promise, was a rumour of company and delight.

He broke into a clearing, running through dead bracken and crisp-stemmed heather. A small she-otter lay on the bank, in the thin rays of the February sunshine. She lifted her head, brown-eyed, alluring. She was smaller than he, silken and slender. She was beauty. She was an otter goddess and sheer perfection. She was all he had ever desired.

Shala stopped and looked at her, and she looked back and fluted to him. She had been lonely too.

That night, two otters ran side by side through the woods. When they came to the sea they dived over and under one another, rolling together in an ecstasy of playfulness, chasing through the waves. Shala caught a fish and shared it with the little female, giving her the first choice bites.

When morning came they were curled together, pressed close, tail to nose and nose to tail, sleeping till the moon called them out again to play on the lonely beach while mankind slept.

One Perfect
Day

ONE PERFECT DAY

Auld Lexie woke early. He looked at the sunshine spilling across the patchwork cover. He looked at the grey cat that lay, smokehaze soft, curled into the small of his back. The cat woke, stared with wide green eyes, stretched and purred, rolling as the old man's hand stroked the soft fur of her underparts.

It was a morning ritual, necessary to both of them. Lexie smiled. Outside, the birds sang to the rising sun. Inside, all was warmth and contentment. The cat jumped to the rocking-chair and sat on chintz cushions, purring to herself while Lexie shaved and dressed. The chair rocked to her movements and this, too, was part of the ritual.

She had come into his life three years before, lost and lonely, strayed from far away. She had forgotten her earlier home; had forgotten the terror she felt when the red fox chased her, and she ran, as no cat ever ran before, over moor and sandy beach and up the path of the little cottage into the arms and heart of the old man who sat in his rocking-chair on the tiny flower-covered porch and held out his arms.

Milk and a gentle voice had soothed her. Lexie asked everyone, but no one knew her and, honour satisfied, he kept her. She brought him immense pleasure, as his old dog had just died and he had not wanted to start a new pup, not at his age. His grandchildren were grown now and there would soon be great-grandchildren, and it was not wise. But he could not live without animals about him.

He walked into the little room that was kitchen and dining-room, that was bright with red tiles on the floor and curtains the colour of the rising sun at the windows. The table was laid with a red check cloth, a yellow cup and saucer and plates, a beehive honeypot and a milk jug on which was a fat Jersey cow, painted so real that Lexie fingered it lovingly, remembering the long years spent with the herd he had thought of as his, though they belonged to the Gaffer. The Gaffer had given him the milk jug on the old man's retirement, but Lexie still walked over the hill to visit the daughters of 'his' cows. He remembered them now.

Bella, who had been so tame she came to meet him in the morning, and showed him her calves with immense pride. And Dorabel, who had been Best in Show at the Royal Show and came home proudly wearing her scarlet rosette, that now hung over Lexie's mantelpiece. A memento from the days when he had worked with the herd, and loved every moment of his work.

Out with the cattle in the dewy morning, with the birds singing. There were more birds then, he thought, as he poured the rich Jersey milk that the Gaffer sent him daily. More birds and more beasts, and life was kinder too.

He fed frugally, eating porridge, prunes sweetened with honey, and a slice of toast. He stood and cleared the dishes, a fine old man, his white hair thick, his figure still tall and erect, his tanned face clean-shaven and gentle, the brown eyes always smiling. He had a way with the beasts all his own, had Lexie, knowing without telling when they were ill or well, knowing how they felt, knowing how to climb, in his thoughts, inside an animal's skin, so that he had no need to be told when a horse was about to bolt, or a cow to butt, or a bull to roar and rush in sudden challenge and toss and stamp in fury.

He could check a child in tantrum and bring peace to any home. His grandchildren adored him. He paused for a moment in his work and fingered the flute that lay on the window-sill where parsley, mint and thyme grew in earthenware pots. The flute was worn with fingering to a rich glowing sheen that winked in the sunshine. The old hands stroked it as if it were alive. Almost, he lifted it to his lips. But there was work to do, and he washed the dishes instead, putting off the morning's pleasures.

An hour later, the cottage so trim that any woman would have been proud, Auld Lexie stepped outside. No trace of wind shivered the grasses or bowed the trees, or ruffled the water of the tiny loch that mirrored the blue sky. It was a perfect morning.

Auld Lexie knew all the signs. He could not read without glasses, but his longsight was perfect. His wise eyes caught a flicker of movement at the edge of the wood. There was a movement in the grass. He smiled again.

The stags were massing for the autumn rut. As yet, they were friends, moving in a herd, untroubled by any passion. The hinds summered in the wood, far away from their masters, guarding the tiny calves until they were big enough to defend themselves against fox and wild cat and eagle, by running fleetly.

There was another telltale movement. There were fifteen full-grown stags lying in the long grass, chewing the cud.

Their many-pronged antlers looked like the branches of long-dead trees. They shone in the sunshine, stripped clean of protecting velvet, proclaiming that the stags were grown and ready for mastery. Now the beasts lay at peace, chewing the cud, their brown-red bodies blending with the ground. Only when they moved their heads could Lexie see them.

He took his flute. He had an appointment to keep with another creature, and the wild beasts were slaves to habit, keeping to the same ways and the same times and the same places. A tremor of excitement quickened his old man's pace as he walked through the heather. He had waited, he had planned, and today he was sure, he would achieve a long-standing ambition. If only he took enough care.

Sunshine gilded the mountains at the head of the loch. He left the heather for the spiky grass that grew at the edge of the stony beach. There were cushions of sea thrift and sea pink, and he bent to pick up the shining round-oval shell of a long-dead sea urchin. His youngest grand-daughter would love it to put on her mantelpiece. She lived away from home, in her first flat, and she longed to be back by the edge of the sea, where the winds blew clean from the smokeless sky. Auld Lexie sent her shells. He was no hand at writing letters, but the little gifts spoke for him. This would need to be packed with extra care; it was eggshell brittle, but it was perfect. It was a treasure. He laid it on the tiny sea wall, lest he should drop it and it broke.

A salmon leaped, body arched and splendid, gleaming silver in the sunshine. Ripples widened, eddying outwards, and then dying until the water was once more still. Lexie trod carefully. The beach was rugged, flinty hard, covered in boulders that might roll and throw him. Behind him came movement and he turned his head. He was amused to see the little cat running, her tail erect. She wove her-self in and out of his legs, purring, and then went to fish in a rock pool and forgot him, as she sat, eyes totally intent, waiting for movement. She specially loved the fairy shrimps, fragile and transparent, that flicked through the water.

Auld Lexie saw many things that morning. He saw the sea otter standing over his kill, eating it on the rocks. The little beast caught the old man's scent, the scent of soap, shaving-cream and tobacco and, lifting his head, saw the intruder, and was gone, melting like dew in the morning.

Lexie sat, waiting, and saw the wildcat with her lean long legs and bushy tail, as she streaked across the wide sandy beach seeking cover. For all her fierce nature, she preferred to hide from man.

He saw the herons fishing. Six of them, spaced like grey sentinels round the loch, feathered shoulders humped, wings folded, crests raised, eyes watching the shallow water that sparkled with a million lights. A beak flashed downwards. A head lifted. The catch was swallowed. The bird was still again, watching quietly.

Lexie moved on, trying to soften the sound of his feet on the ridged grey-granite rocks. The herons rose heavily, wingbeats thunderous on the still air, and flapped towards the distant trees on the other side of the water.

The old man edged carefully onto a spit of rock that jutted into the water. He lived alone and prided himself on his ability to look after himself, troubling no other man. He would not risk a tumble in the sea, where the chill might shock his old man's bones and give him pneumonia or, worse, a twist of the leg that might break a bone. He seated himself on the warm stones. The placid water hid its teeth and splashed softly in creaming folds some feet beneath him.

The tide was filling, but the rock was always well above high water, and even at flood he was safe here and could make his way back. He knew the perils of being cut off by the sea, and had many times rescued foolish summer visitors, using the sturdy, heavy clinker-built boat that he now kept on a long line, bobbing on the water. He could no longer drag it up and down the beach.

He took the flute from the tiny knapsack that protected

it and handled it with gnarled brown fingers, bent with rheumatism, worn with long years of tending his cattle. He sighed suddenly, wishing he were young again, in his pomp again, a proud man, striding the fields, while the caramel-coloured cows lowed behind him and he could sit, twice daily, on his stool at the milking, singing softly, using his hands as God meant man to use them, not trusting the cold cups of the machines that took away all the pleasure from herding.

He remembered the soft song he sang and hummed it again.

> *Cushy, cushy, little coo, little coo milking,*
> *Cushy, cushy, leave your milk, little coo milking.*
> *Cushy, cushy, lean on me, let me have your milk noo,*
> *Cushy, cushy, little coo, your hide is soft as silk, noo.*

It had been a daft rhyme, a nonsense rhyme, taught him long ago by his own grandfather. Perhaps he had made it up himself, or had maybe been taught it by his grandfather. There had always been a Lexie as cooman on Gaffer's farm. But Gaffer was old and had no sons, and when he died the land would go for houses, and that was tragic. It was all change and not for the better, Lexie thought, and whistled a note on the flute, and promptly forgot these thoughts, as old men forget, and saw only the morning. Time was his, as was the whole world, the quiet empty beach and the sandbank out at sea, half hidden by the rising tide, the tiny waves sucking at the sand's edge and then retreating.

He blew again into the mouthpiece. Rounded notes floated over the loch, and he forgot his age and the pains of old bones as he used all his skill to work brain and mouth and fingers together, and the soft notes echoed over the dancing water.

Auld Lexie played his tunes and waited. He watched the quiet surface, then satisfaction shone in his eyes as the seals came, their heads lifted to listen. They floated up from the rocky crags that lay deep under water. They came from distant beaches where they lay with their young. The black seals had borne their pups in the spring. The grey seals were pupping now, before the autumn gales blew strong and the waves crashed in fury for days on end and the sea was wicked.

The seals came from the deep, drifting beds of tangled weed. They came from the deep ravine in the centre of the loch. They slid off the rocks and swam towards the music, yearning for its wonderful tone, for the soothing caress of the notes that soared towards the sky and drowned the bird noise.

Auld Lexie played a lilt, a lilt for the flower time and the young girls picking flowers for garlands. And he played a lament, for the young men gone to war and never returning. He played a reel, and set the waves dancing and the birds singing in sudden joy, seeking to outdo him. And then he played a lullaby, the song that Mary sang to the Christ baby as he lay against her, his tiny hands curling and uncurling like small sea creatures, as he listened.

> *Hush, my little one, hush.*
> *All is peace.*
> *Sleep, my little one, sleep,*
> *Let care now cease.*

Sleep, my little king, sleep.
All is still.
Stay, my little prince, stay.
Peace, be still.

The soft notes died away, and the birdsong quietened. Auld Lexie watched the herd come closer. He had played to them for years and he knew them all. He saw the black bull heave himself from the water, and noted a new scar across the broad wrinkled brow. The Auld One had been fighting again. Lexie saw the grey seal with the brown eyes that gleamed like twin suns. She had a brand new calf beside her, and she nosed him and he butted her with his big head that was so out of proportion on the small body.

The morning warmed to midday. Lexie played on, trying to still the excitement that was mastering him and making his fingers uncertain. Today, he was sure, his dream would come true. He lifted the flute again and played a quick, gay, rippling air of running notes that soared above him and were picked up by the birds again. They were heard by the wildcat, who had crouched to listen, by the otter that had stopped beside the mouth of the little burn that spilled into the sea, and by the little cat that paused in her fishing, but then went on because a tail flashed in the sunshine and her instincts could not be denied.

The listening seals swam closer. Lexie remained still, although the muscles of his legs were cramped and knotted. Only his mobile red-lipped mouth, moving fingers and brilliant eyes were alive.

He saw her coming. She was sleek and young and
beautiful and no bull yet owned her. She had come daily,
for weeks, to hear the music. Lexie changed to a wild tune,
a tune that spoke of the sea, of the rolling breakers surging
towards the rocks, of the small waves creaming, of the
wind lulling on a sunny day, strengthening to a gale, send-
ing the ships running for harbour and the white-winged
gulls flying willowy-winged to inland lakes and peace.

The little seal was enthralled. She forgot the wariness of
all creatures that hide in the deep waters. She pulled herself out of the sea, muscles rippling. Her sleek skin shone.
Her brown eyes glowed. Her body quivered with ecstasy
as the music folded her in enchantment.

Lexie played on, afraid to break the spell, adapting the

music, now soft, now louder, now soothing, now calling, enticing her towards him, moving slowly, pulled by invisible yearnings, towards the sound that ensnared her, the sound that she did not understand, but that gave her feelings she had never known before. Lexie did not know it, but he was playing as the sirens played, long ago, and the music was irresistible.

She was so close he could see the milky light in her brown eyes as she yearned at him. She was so close he could see the whiskers that came, catlike, from her cheeks. She was so close he could see the shine of sun on her sleek and gleaming pelt. She was so close that he could see the quiver of her throat as she breathed and the widening of her nostrils. He could not take his eyes from her, but he was careful not to stare straight at her, knowing that this was something all animals hated.

After a while she began to make a deep, strange sound, almost a full-throated purr. Her wide eyes stared opaquely, her head and shoulders swayed in rhythmic pleasure. She came closer still, and closer, and Lexie felt her body wet against his ankles, leaning on his legs, and delight so thrilled him that he almost broke into a paean of excitement. He mastered the impulse and played on, softly and soothingly, holding her against him by the music, savouring every second, knowing for the first time the utter and uncommunicable achievement that a man gains when a creature of the wild trusts him.

The sun was shadowed by a tiny cloud.

Footsteps crashed on the shore. A magpie yickered irritably, calling a warning that was echoed by all the other birds. The wildcat fled, the otter hid, the woods cleared. A tail slapped the water and the seals were gone.

Lexie pocketed his flute. He stood, cramps shooting through his legs. He walked stiffly home, an old man, on a grey day, the sun gone, it seemed, almost for ever. Behind him, children ran and called on the beach, commenting on its emptiness, not knowing that before they came it had been busier than they would ever imagine. No eyes looked from the woods. No head broke the now ruffled waters.

Lexie did not notice the chill. He did not feel the pains, or the stiffness, or the cramp that held his arm and made his old legs falter. He floated over the heather, ecstatic. Success was his at last. In all his years, no seal had ever come so close, or trusted him so that she leaned against him. He could still feel the pressure of her body and his trouser leg was wet where she had rested.

The grey cat ran through the wood and joined him, leaping to his shoulder and perching there against his face, as he walked the last few steps home. His lips smiled in secret delight, and the day remained, to stay in memory for ever, bathed in sunlight, a day of purest pleasure, of absolute perfection.

He put away the flute and fed the cat, and ate his own sparse meal. He dozed the afternoon away and dreamed of seals that played around him, and came to listen to his flute. He was one among them and, when the day ended, he swam with them, far from land, and dived in deep water—and was young again and strong.

The cat slept on his lap and she, too, purred.

The Secret
Herds

There were two watchers on the hill. High above the tree level, looking down the long sweep of pine trees and coarse grass to the distant shimmer that was the wind-troubled loch, the eagle stood, poised, a feathered engine of destruction.

Beyond him, in the nest, were two clamorous young, their screams for food urgent in his brain. The nest was large, an untidy jumble of interwoven twigs and branches that his mate had camouflaged with the torn green leafy twigs of growing trees, that also lent a little shelter to the young. The mountain loured above, fierce-cragged, often hidden in cloud. No man could ever reach the nest, nor could the wildcat, the eagle's only enemy.

Time and again he winged wearily over the wood, swooped to the rocky barrens that edged the sea, and sped nestwards, bearing scanty comfort to the growing fledglings whose ever-open beaks asked for food and yet more food, and whose raucous cries angered the windy air.

There were other watchers in the woods. The wildcat crouched where the tumbled rocks met the trees, and the bracken offered shelter. Her immense body was striped and barred, her wicked offset ears were flat, her thick blunt tail swept in anger. Her glowing eyes were wide and eager and saliva filled her mouth. Behind her, in a gnarl of rock, safe from wind and rain and intruding crow, her unweaned catlings lay, calling to her, demanding her return. Already, they asked for more than her body could supply. The winter had been longer than usual and mortal hard, a wild time of blizzard and long-lying snow, and ice that bit deep into the rivers and lakes. It bit, too, into the bones of the tiny creatures that could not hide from the wind's cruel teeth.

Both wildcat and eagle had one object in mind. The red deer calf that lay in the bracken, unaware of observation, was sturdy, but not yet ready to run. After the birth was over and the hind had cleared his coat, she nosed him, pushing him down, anxious to ensure that he was well hidden in the long rough grass that she had chosen for his resting place, where bracken thrust through the tangled roots and helped to hide the little one. But the flies were persistent and tormenting, and the flicker of his ears as he tried to shake them off betrayed them to both wildcat and eagle.

Beyond him, the main herd fed, many calves already active, skipping at their mother's side. The Auld Yin, the great great great-grandmother of the new calf, watched for danger. Danger, that could come from the two-legged creatures with the extraordinary fur and the frightening sticks that spat fire, and brought quick death to the fortunate, and slow torture to the unlucky if a bullet struck a leg and maimed instead of killing. Danger, that could come from the spitting wildcat; danger, that could plunge from the innocent sky in a wildness of wings, tearing talons and desperate beak.

The Auld Yin heard the soft rustle of the feeding herd, the plash and play of far-away waves on the rocky beach, the plangent sound of crooning gulls, and the sigh of the wind in the shivering trees. A bird cried a shrill note of alarm.

The sky was alive with falling wings, with the beating thrust of muscles anxious to kill. The plummeting body broke the blue, the Auld Yin stamped, the herd, startled, turned to flee, the outliers already crashing noisily through the underbrush.

The new mother ran to her calf. Here, she knew, was the message that had pulled the bird towards them. As the bird plunged, the Auld Yin too came to the rescue. The other hinds watched and milled in scared confusion, while the calves hid in thick cover, in the bramble and bracken brakes beneath the trees.

The new calf had no knowledge of life or danger, but instincts bred in him showed him how to lie against the ground, sprawled as if dead, not moving a hoof, or flicking an ear, his head outstretched, his eyes wide, ignoring even the teasing flies.

Talons reached towards the tempting body that would bring rest to the exhausted eagle. It would last for hours, enabling him also to feed well for the first time for days. He could feed his weary mate, and thrust good meat into the crops of the two young birds that bound him to them with fetters more potent than any he had ever known. They were his first children, and he was young.

The Auld Yin turned her back. As the outstretched talons clawed, her speeding hooves took the eagle in the chest, tossed him off balance, and the younger hind, tucking her own legs underneath her tail, caught him a double kick that sent him, frustrated and aching, to the shelter of a high tree, where he recovered his breath and preened his ruffled feathers.

At that moment, the wildcat sprang.

Body arched, she landed on the calf, claws clinging. The Auld Yin stamped again in fury and turned, enraged, to battle, her first kick unbalancing the cat. The mother deer, savage, all instincts roused in defence of her young, caught the cat in the ribs, so that she turned, snarling, bruised and aching, but still hungry and determined.

She crouched, facing her enemies, little wildcat, braver than the mountain lion, now all angry savaging hunger-ache. She was fierce with the need to feed the kittens that she cherished more than life.

A rising wind keened through the branches, banshee-wailing down the long wet slopes. The eagle huddled, hurt, in the tree, his eyes seeing the fight, watching for the small life that shivered in the grass where tiny mouse and shrew hid, fearing the battle, fearing the cat and fearing the bird. All around the air reeked of enemies.

A bird chanted, a monotonous, nerve-tingling danger call. Cat! Cat! Cat! Beyond it others took up the sound until the wood was alive with terror, sounding in bellnotes and chatters, in screech and click and chuck and jaycall. High on the hill the solitary stags moved to safety, listening fearfully, unaware that the hinds faced danger while the masters of the hill lived untroubled by family care.

The spitting wildcat launched herself in fury at the Auld Yin. The calf, aching from his scratches, one ear bleeding, lifted his head. His mother stood over him. He smelled her warm milky udder and began to feed, all fear forgotten in the comfort of her presence.

The Auld Yin, the cat clinging to her back, hanging on with gripping teeth and clinging claws, sped towards the water, her fur, like that of the calf, protecting her from most of the fury. She was old and waywise and this was not the first time she had tangled with the little tiger of the hills. She raced downhill, not even trying to shake the she-cat from her grip. Speeding hooves cleared rocky tump and heather clump, the beating rush startling every animal that heard it so that birds winged fast to safety and small beasts cowered and hid.

The old hind leaped a trickling crystal beck where water chuckled over the tiny shingle and minnows lurked in the rain-specked whirls. Below her, she saw her target, a

vast old tree, its branches low and spreading, and she hurled herself towards it, just missing the big bough that protruded over the water, dislodging the cat which clung fervently to the flaking bark, while the Auld Yin bounded again and turned to run over the grassy track that led uphill towards the waiting, anxious herd.

The wildcat would not be baulked. She dropped to earth and raced along on the scented track, a ball of fluffed fury with death in her heart. The eagle saw her and plunged. She leaped sideways as he came. He missed and his talons tore the earth and, before he could regain height and plunge again, she had vanished, smokehaze fast, and was no more than a memory on the wind. That day, she and the kittens fed on fish which she caught in the beck, and on small mice, hidden in the long grass.

The eagle found a dead lamb, flung down in the field for the shepherd to bury when he had time to spare. He had none now, as the lambs were coming fast. This one had died at birth, and it fed the young eagles and both parents. The two birds rested, the father sleeping, head beneath his wing, while the mother brooded the young and watched clouds gather about her and the rain soak from the sky, chilling everything about them.

The eagle woke when the moon was high. Poised above the nest, he watched the haunting owl, anxious to feed his own featherlings. The moon stencilled a pattern on the fluffing white tendrils that edged the receding tide, and on the dapple-patterned back of the wildcat, who had taken her kittens for their first outing. They played, unaware of the eyes high above them, tapping at drifting weed that blew, brittle dry on the wind, and patting too at grass stems and a moth that bumbled across their path.

The still waters hid a seal, feeding on a salmon. Small dramas were enacted every hour. On the hillside a lurking poacher brooded too, godlike, knowing that in the wild no creature may relax, for the lawless take what they must where they may in order to live, and there is no pity.

The Wild Horses

Long ago, before the Roman Eagles were carried high over Britain, forests and swamps masked the land. Wolf and bear vied with foxes and, in the woods, the little hardy horses ran wild, their foals at heel, and no man ever mastered them. Men watched them from afar, as they watched all wild creatures, but the horses were very wild. And they kicked.

In the southern part of Britain, a boy lived with his tribe. He was small and dark and dressed in wolfskins. They called him Edda. He was an odd boy, able to run faster than any other boy in the tribe, able to swim under water and hold his breath longer, able to shoot with his bow and arrow and knock a tiny shell from the top of a flat rock with the flinthead.

Yet he did not want to run or swim or shoot with the other boys. He felt more at ease in the forest where he spent much of his time alone. He knew where the wolf laired, and watched the cubs at play. He knew where the big bear had her den, and watched her teach her young to fish. She was very clever. Her big paws flipped the fish onto the bank and the babies fought for them. Fish grew much bigger in those long ago days.

Edda's father was always angry.

That night, the night that the boy was to remember for all of his life, Edda crouched on his haunches at the back of the big cave. His father was the chieftain's son, and his family had the right to the best dwelling of all, after the chieftain himself. Edda sat behind the fire. Woodsmoke filled the air, and his little sister coughed. She was small and thin and sickly, and was always coughing.

Now Edda glowered at his father. The hateful words stung and cut, and were all too familiar. All the same, he could not change. He rubbed his short strong fingers through the little badger's coat, feeling the stiff hairs, alive and warm, beneath them.

Edda was proud of the little badger. The old male had been trapped, but the boy had rescued this little cub and tamed her, so that she now followed him everywhere. No beasts ever followed other members of the tribe. They threw stones at the wild dogs that came boldly and hungrily to the cave entrances, looking for bones. They threw stones at the wildcats that flew in, stole food and raced out again, but were tolerated because they caught the rats that plagued the caves, feeding on food that was left over and never buried or thrown away.

The cats and dogs were far too savage to touch. They were almost as wild as the wicked little horses that bucked on the hills. Yet the badger followed Edda, and the other members of his tribe eyed the boy uneasily, fearing that he was a wizard and the badger his evil spirit conjured from the ghosts of the dead. Edda was a strange boy. Even his eyes were strange, glowing eyes of deep brown-amber, more like a beast's eyes than a man's. The old women muttered and moved away when he came, and spat to placate the wood demons who were surely guarding this oddling that lived among them and had a wild beast follow him more closely than a baby followed his mother.

'Other men,' Edda's father was saying, 'have strong fierce sons. Sons who kill. You are a fool. The badger is food, and should die to feed your little sister. The hunting is bad this year. Look at your mother's sister's son, Harda. He is the same age as you, yet already he has killed a wolf and strangled a bear cub with his hands. You have never killed one single animal, even with a knife.'

Edda clenched his jaw and dug his fingers into the loose skin at the back of the badger's neck. Angered, she turned and bit him, administering a sharp reproof. He sucked at the blood. He had deserved her warning.

'I am the chieftain's son and will one day be chieftain, and you will come after me,' Edda's father said. He aimed a savage kick with his bare foot at the unburnt end of a blazing log. Fire leaped and shadows danced on the cave walls.

'I cannot face the other men around the camp fire at night,' Edda's father said. He aimed an angry fist at his son. 'You disgrace me.'

Edda held the badger close against him and backed into the darkness. The rough damp wall was harsh against the bare skin of his shoulder.

'Get out,' his father shouted. 'Do not return until you can prove you are a man!'

Edda snatched a lump of meat from the cave floor and ran outside. He knew his mother would be no protection. His father was a fierce and impatient man, and it was never wise to argue with him. The tribal laws were harsh, but could not be disobeyed. Edda knew that, if he did not soon prove his manhood and kill one of the prowling wolves that terrified the caves and killed the game that should have fed the people, he would be barred from the tribe and left to fend for himself in the woods and forests, the target of any stray stones that the other boys might throw.

He left without a backward glance. There was a small cave, hidden under the roots of a big hollow tree, where he could put the little badger for safety. It would not be the first time. She might dig herself out, but she had not done so before. He pushed her inside and masked the doorway with a rock to keep out hunting beasts that might kill her, and left her half his meat to chew. He needed to be free, to run if need be, to kill if he must. His only weapons were his leather sling and a small store of rounded pebbles, and a sharp-edged flint knife.

He needed sleep. He ran among the trees and climbed high, out of the way of wolf and bear. He dozed uneasily, aware of the creak of trunks and the rustle of leaves and the haunting cry of the wind, that was the mouthpiece of the demons that rode through the night and savaged the forest. Often, in the morning, they had torn great branches from the trees, when their servant the gale blew his terrible anger. Once they had sent sheet lightning into the woods and destroyed a giant tree that must have disobeyed them. All the tribe knew that spirits lived in the trees and mastered them.

Edda woke when the moon slid out of the sky. The morning was wild, great clouds banked in soaring pyramids into a sky that was as grey as the grey wolf that he knew laired in the clearing beyond the little lake where the salmon swam at spawning time. They lay in the mouth of the stream, where it fed the lake, running swiftly over a pebble bed of clear green pebbles, weed-masked, the weed astream in the water like the River Maid's hair. Edda was much more afraid of the wrath of the spirits than he was of the teeth of the beasts that lurked in the wild ways. He sighed deeply and watched the thin rays of the sun filter through cloud and lighten the ground.

Below him, clear of his scent, a vixen played with her cubs. That he could understand. He spent so much time in the woods, and knew the track of every four-footed beast and of some of the birds. He could see where the otter had crouched to eat, where the bear had sharpened his claws, where the wolf had lain at night, where the wild mare had borne her foal. One of the otter cubs came to his whistle. Often, he watched it slide in the water and play with the shadows that patterned the ground, trying to catch the sunshine flicker cast between dancing leaves.

Edda dropped from the tree. He went to the stream where the fat trout lay beneath the edge of the bank. He knelt and, slowly, gently, scarcely moving his hand, slid his fingers under one of the somnolent creatures and stroked its underbelly. The soothing touch was mesmeric; the fish flicked a lazy tail, holding itself with the current, unaware of danger. Slowly, slowly, gently, softly, and then the fingers flashed into the opening gills and the fish was on the bank, gasping.

Edda hit it against a stone and ate it raw, wiping his slimy hands and mouth with grass torn from the river bank. He sat, hunched, thinking and wondering. Beyond him was the downland, where the cushion moss was soft and flowers starred the green. The waving grass rippled in the wind, and he caught his breath as four wild ponies flew away from him, manes rising in the wind, long streamer tails behind them.

They turned. They were running for joy, running for fun, loving freedom, safely out of danger from the wolf pack that had killed and gone, seeking other prey. They bowed their heads to drink, necks arched and slender. Brown eyes glowed as they looked towards Edda, but he was lost, was a blur of wolfskin in the grass, so still that they did not see him or heed him. He gloried in their movements. He saw the wind playing with their manes and tails, saw the wild brown eyes alert for wolf signs, saw the sudden stampede as the herd broke towards him, wheeled, turned and fled for safety, and the four drinkers followed, their hooves drumming on the hard ground.

All fled except one. The little mare lay alone, her eyes terrified. She was about to foal. She watched the lone prowler that had panicked her fellows. He circled, lips snarling, teeth bared, ready to spring.

Edda did not pause to think. He had his knife with him, a stone knife, the edge honed to such keenness that it could cut through sinew as it could cut through a leaf. He sprang, coming sideways to the hunter, and the blade cut the big neck vein and the wolf died at once. Edda had obeyed the tribal custom without even thinking. He severed the tail as proof of his prowess and turned to more important matters.

The foal was born, but both mare and young were exhausted. She could not rise and run and the baby lay beside her, unable to move. Edda saw that it was not breathing. Its head was covered in the birth membrane as the mother had not managed to free the nostrils. Edda crept up to her, knowing how frightened she must be. He took the knife and the mare struggled to stand, and he hissed at her, softly and soothingly, and cut through the clear covering that kept the air from the foal. There was still no flicker of life and, as the mother nosed it, she began to whicker, a soft cry of grief that Edda could not bear.

He bent to the foal, and breathed life into its nostrils, but the foal did not respond. He took his knife and cut a strip from the edge of his tunic and began to rub the little animal as he had seen his mother rub his small sister. She too had not breathed or cried when she was born.

Rub. Rub. Rub. He was aching with effort. He was so tired he could not go on. He put the fur-piece down on the ground, and the mother reached out her head and began to lick, as if recognizing that he had been trying to help her. Lick. Lick. Lick.

The foal drew in a deep convulsive breath, and let it out again with a small cry. The mare stood, swaying on her long legs and continued licking. The foal was moving. He was moving his small tail. He was flickering his small ears. He was trying to stand on his thin long unsteady legs. Edda brought water in his cupped hands, and the mare drank.

He lifted the foal, showing it how to suck. He had never known such intense pleasure before. He had felt nothing when he killed the wolf, not the thrust of manhood pride of which the older boys boasted, not the pleasure of a kill, nor any achievement. It had been necessary and he regretted the need.

This was different. The mare took grass from his fingers, and the foal trusted him, even as his little badger trusted him. This was total achievement, a mastery such as no other man had ever known. He tucked the wolftail in his belt. He could go home now, and his father could brag round the campfire that his son too was a man. But the mare could not run yet, or fight, and her foal was helpless, and so too was she. He saw when she moved that there was a gash on her shoulder, as if some animal had already attempted to take her. He rubbed the wound clean to keep the flies from it and spread it with the Healing Leaves, as the wise man did the war wounds of the tribe.

He collected brushwood and made the Fire Magic, rubbing the sticks as the Wise Man rubbed them. It was not allowed, but perhaps the Great Ones who lived in the sky and roared their anger in thunder rumbles would forgive him, for his need was great. He would nurse the mare and tame her, and the fire would keep the wolves at bay.

He spoke to the mare. She learned to trust him, to come when he whistled softly, and the foal, having known Edda from birth, did not know that he should be afraid. The foal was coal black and followed Edda as often as he followed his mother.

Edda fed on fish and on the roots of the Safe Plants, and on mushrooms that grew in a clearing and that he grilled on a stick over the fire that he kept burning night and day. Rank woodsmoke plumed on the air and no wild killer came near.

At the end of three weeks Edda wove a rope of strong twine, pulling the long thin leaves of the rushes and twisting them together, twining them to strengthen them with thin sappy long twigs torn from the willows. When the rope was made to his satisfaction he haltered the mare. She disliked the feeling, but within the space of a day she was resigned.

Two days later, she followed him through the forest, the foal beside her. Their journey was very slow. Edda watched for enemies, and dared not sleep lest wolves came and killed the mare and her foal.

Early next morning Edda and the two horses crossed a little stream, where grey boulders lay under chuckling water that thrust and sped on its way to the river. A stone slipped and Edda fell. His foot twisted beneath him. He had never known such pain. He stood, sickened, holding on to the mare's mane for support, feeling her warm against him, her breath hot on his cheek. Tears stung his eyes.

He hobbled to the bank and sat on a rock. The mare gazed. The foal suckled. Edda watched his ankle swell. The skin was blue and yellow and puffy. He could not walk. He could not move. They were not safe. He could not protect them. He needed to get back to the tribe. He needed help. There was no help.

He built a new fire. If he stayed close to the river he could fish. He had no choice. He rested, while the sprain eased and the wet leaves he bound with grass around his ankle soothed the burning pain that seemed to be with him all day and all night.

Summer was now full blown and the days were warm and sunny. Edda found a large hollow under a tree and slept there, curled like an animal, with the mare and foal beside him. The hollow was warm and held the sun, and the grass was good. The mare grew sleek and the foal grew tall and leggy as the days went by.

One night a wolf came. The mare whinnied and Edda leaped from the branch of a tree to the beast's back and killed it and took the tail. He too had grown, a little in height, a great deal in confidence. He was not in need of help from the tribe. He could live alone, if he chose. He did not choose. He was a man and there was a girl, slender as the foal and gentle. He remembered her with longing. She had never looked at him before. He was no hero, no wolf killer.

Now he had two tails to offer her, and he had more than the other boys in the tribe.

One morning, when the sun was high on the hills, and the birds calling, he backed the mare. She threw him to the ground, furious at such impudence. Edda climbed on her back again. And again. And again.

That was enough. He left her in peace, but next day when he mounted once more she was slower to throw him off. She endured him, very briefly. He was more patient than the fishing heron. He persisted, day after long day, until she allowed him to stay. Then he nudged her with his heels and she moved forward. He learned to ride her, to ride her at a walk, a trot, a canter, and then at a head-long gallop, pelting over the turf, her drumming hooves a wild excitement.

This was joy. This was exultation. This was achievement. Never before in all of man's history had a horse been ridden.

When the first frost rimed the grasses, he rode his mare

through the forests. The foal followed. They came to the campfire at dusk when the men were sleepy with fermented honey and talked loudly, laughing and bragging of their victories against the other tribes in the forest, and against the wolf and bear and wild boar.

They looked up and saw a bronzed, tall lad on a dark bay mare. She huffed at them and walked forward as Edda dug in his heels. She was very wary, but she already knew fire, and these men smelled as Edda smelled. She would not approach close, but the foal went forward and stood, ears pricked, and stared at them.

No one recognized Edda. He had grown enormously in height in the summer months, having reached the growing age. He was darkened by the sun, and he was proud. His long hair was bleached by sunshine. He looked down at them, a small smile on his lips. They were such little men, seen from his height. They sprang to their feet, and made the age-old gesture to ward off evil. Truly, this was a spirit come to them, or a demon, or a wizard, with his attendants. No man could ever sit upon a wild animal's back.

Edda jumped down.

He took the mare's halter, urging her forward, until they stood in the campfire's gleam. The foal was alarmed by the men's sudden movement and he stood between Edda and his mother, watching.

'It is I, Edda.'

He swaggered forward a few paces and flung the wolf tails at his father's feet. He did not wait to hear the exclamations. He turned towards an empty cave at the top of the hill and took it as his right, taking both mare and foal inside with him. He went to the hollow tree. The badger had gone, having dug her way out long ago, but when he whistled she came from the bushes and nosed him joyfully. She had not forgotten him. Behind her came three cubs and Edda grinned and rubbed her broad nose, and left her with her family, aware of a suspicious boar watching him from the undergrowth.

Edda made a bed of dry leaves for the mare and her foal, and brought in grass, cut with his knife, and flung it to her. She fed. Three small boys watched from the doorway of the cave, and one came forward bringing large pieces of roast bear, cooked over the fire in his mother's cave, for Edda. This was a hero, a man of two wolf tails, a man whom the singers would honour, a man who had ridden one of the wildest creatures on earth. They looked at him, awestruck, and Edda smiled inside himself, pleased to be greeted with such admiration, but aware that he was very little different from the Edda who went out. He still would not kill, except from sheer necessity.

Late that night Edda's father came to the cave.

'I see I was wrong,' he said, squatting on his haunches by the fire that the Wise Man had lighted. 'All men have gifts. Some are hunters. Some make sharper weapons than any others. Some know how to work the flint so that the edge is swift to kill, and sure. Others fish. But never has the tribe known one like you. You can charm the wild creatures and make them tame.'

He stopped and looked at Edda.

'Tame horses for all the tribe. That is your manhood work, your place among us. When we can all ride as swiftly as the wild horses that race against the wind, then we will be the most powerful tribe in all the world. Our men will rule all other tribes.'

He bent and swiftly carved the manhood scars on Edda's face. Blood dripped from the V-shaped slash on either cheek.

Edda watched his father climb down the rocks. His eyes were exultant. The tribe would ride the wild horses in all the years to come and he, Edda, would master them.

From the campfire, he heard the crier call his manhood name.

'We drink to Edda, the bringer of wild horses, the tamer of wild animals, the One Whose Dreams Come True.'

Edda smiled in the firelight glow. He sat beside the sleeping mare and fondled her mane and dreamed of the day he would lead his tribe to victory riding a stallion such as no man had ever seen in all his days. Was he not Edda, the first man in the world to ride a horse?

The Peregrine

'You can go out if you're careful,' his mother had said.

Davie looked about him. He had spent all the long winter in hospital, and now it was spring, and he was free. He sat on a rock in the sunshine and hugged his legs.

It was a warm day. The sun had strength and glowed on the newly opening buds on the trees. Everything was so bright after the white walls and white beds of the long ward where the days had passed so slowly, broken only by meal times and visitors. Then, days seemed endless. Now they passed so fast.

There were woods below him. Woods where the trees shone with brilliance, where green glowed to gold, and yellow ripened to russet. He had never realized there was so much colour in the buds. Through the forest an ash showed its white trunk, the black buds still close and secret.

There were windflowers under the trees, white-petalled, veined with black, hanging bell-like on thin stems so fragile that they swung in the smallest breeze. There were yellow coltsfoot starring the grass, and celandines, wet-shining petals waxy gold.

There was bird noise, high in the air. Twitter and chirp, and the warning wariness of a scolding blackbird as one of the house cats came near. Davie called her. She was ginger striped and fat with a round head and green eyes that stared at him. She pushed against his hand, weaved her body round his legs and her deep purr delighted him. He had missed the animals almost more than the people when he was in hospital. His mother and father were so busy and his older brother so much older than he.

There had always been the cats and dogs, the young spring lambs and the calves to play with. There had been tiny yellow chicks and absurd goslings that followed him wherever he went. Those he missed most of all. He loved the farm. He loved it even more after weeks spent in bed, while his stupid leg refused to heal. He had been knocked off his bicycle by a car that he had not seen, as he turned across a busy road.

Now he was well, except for an ache at night and the need to rest or the ache was almost unbearable. He could not yet run, but by the end of the summer he would be as good as new again, the doctor had told him. Already he could walk without a limp, and take longer strides without the nagging pain to nudge him.

He wanted to hug the woods and the hedgerows that glittered with newly-opened hawthorn flowers. He wanted to run, but that was not yet possible. He wanted to roll, like a colt, and he did, lying on his back on the grass, bicycling his legs up and down, exercising the unwilling muscles.

He sat up again, laughing at himself, and below him, in the Seven Acre field, the two colts frisked together and rolled as he had rolled, flinging their long legs skywards, rubbing their backs against the grass. Then they raced against each other and against the flying shadows that fled before them as they chased down the field, and fled after them as they ran back, challenging each other.

There was a shadow on the grass at his feet. A flying shadow that was faster than the wind itself, and Davie looked up. There, above him, was a peregrine falcon. He stared at it. Peregrines were few in these parts and he had never seen one here before. He had seen them in the zoo. He couldn't be wrong.

The bird was enormous, its wings spread out as it floated on the air. He could see the brown feathering, the creamy bars, the broad tail and the backswept wings. Even as he watched, it beat up the sky, rising higher until it was a dot against the sun, and then it plunged, down, down, down, almost to Davie's head and braked and swept upwards, spiralling. The birds around him cried their fear and anger.

Hawk!

The blackbird was shouting from the hawthorn, his voice sharp and scolding. He flew and hid.

Hawk!

The robin had flown, the only memory of him a shrill twitter, as he cried his warning in his turn. They had been angry at the cat's coming, but nothing like this.

Hawk!

The thrush sat tight on her eggs, her drumming heart beating. She would defy him, fly up at him, challenge him, keep the babies safe. She crouched lower, hiding the faint colour of the warm shells beneath her. There were already sounds from inside. Soon the babies would hatch and she would be busy. Her mate flew into shelter, a worm in his beak, and fed her, and added his voice to the scolding.

Hawk!

The lark hid in the grass. Her young were hatched and she was ready to fly from them, from the nest, lag-winged, limping, teasing the intruder till he chased her far away, leaving the nestlings in safety. Then she would speed into the sky and away to the trees, to lose herself in a maze of branches too dense for the enemy to penetrate. When he had gone, she would return to her brood and feed them.

Hawk!

The pheasant hen ran for cover under the thick bramble. Her fifteen black-striped chicks ran with her, and then crouched motionless under her protecting wing. They were not there at all. They were gone, were invisible, were a blur on the ground, brown and gold and black, blending and merging and hiding. They did not move, not one flick of a feather, while the anger sounded on the terrified air.

Hawk!

The partridges crept into the ditch where the grass grew thickest.

Hawk!

The field mice hid in holes, the shrews vanished, even though they were safe. Only young untried birds ever took them, and then only once, as the reek from their poison glands made for sickness. No bird, no cat and no fox took a shrew a second time. Not to eat.

Hawk!

There were rabbits playing in a grassy clearing. An urgent foot stamped on the ground, white scuts raced for shelter, and the grass was bare. Davie saw the flash of fur and smiled to himself. The rabbits were safe.

Hawk!

The hawk was playing. She was free, and the air was

hers to master. Down the slipstreams and up the thermals, plunging swiftly, soaring towards the sun, beating away from the moor, and returning, not wanting anything but to test her wings and test her speed, and celebrate spring.

She plunged again, and this time Davie caught a tiny tinkle, a faint almost not-there note. He listened harder. The sound came again, sweet, soft and clear. The falcon was belled. She was a tame bird, escaped, perhaps from a zoo, or from some city owner.

If only he could catch her. Could lure her from the sky, could take her home on his fist, could show everyone the bird. This is my falcon. He would name her. What would he name her? The peregrine, the royal bird. He would name her Splendour. She was a splendid bird and it was a splendid name.

He would go back to school and say casually, 'I must get home. I have to feed my falcon. I must feed Splendour, and she needs exercise.'

He would make a lure of rookwings, bait it with meat, tie it to a cord and swing it round his head, once and again, and again. The bird would stand on the air, dive to the lure, seize it in strong talons and land on the ground. Davie would gentle her onto his fist, and walk with the bird balanced and beautiful, a giant bird, a dream of a bird, and all his own.

The peregrine soared again. The angry calls were louder, insistent and repeated. Go away. Go away. Go away. Danger. Danger. Danger. Hawk. Hawk. Hawk.

The blackbird was close to Davie and his scold was deafening. But the boy was so entranced he did not hear.

He was a prince in the Middle Ages, dressed in velvet,

his doublet the blue of a summer sky, his shirt a cream of white lace, his velvet bonnet black, the plume on it sweeping his neck. He wore scarlet stockings and a jewelled belt, and the handle of his dagger was a carved falcon. He was the king's son and all men obeyed him.

This was his falcon, this bird playing, and time had gone back and nothing had changed for centuries. The moors and the trees were as they had always been, all those long years ago. Spring had come then too, and the flowers were the same—the yellow and the white—and the willows were dusted with catkins, then and now.

Time was a river and he had slipped back along the current. There was a falcon behind him, belonging to his mother, and his father the king was as fierce as the eagle he bore on his hand. There were ten birds in the royal mews. Davie had forgotten everything. He was no longer a farmer's son. He stood erect and held his arm out, bound in his school scarf, not seeing the scarf but knowing it was a leather glove made of softest leather, embroidered on the gauntlet.

The bird saw the fist and memory returned to her— memory of the man who had tamed her and fed her. With the knowledge that she was hungry and did not know how to feed herself, and the longing for human company, which was the only company she had known for three whole years, she plunged from the sky.

Down to the swinging lure. Down to the waiting boy. Down to safety. The days alone had been lonely, hungry days, for this bird, born in captivity, had never known the teaching of her parents, had never fled after living prey and caught and killed, had no idea how to hunt for herself.

She was lonely for the man who owned her, and for the sound of a soft voice gentling her, for the safety of a strong arm to bear her, and the food that man brought her, and the close peace of her block at night, in the silent shed far away.

There was memory still, and fear, for one night fire had come from the sky. Flame and a flash and a crash and a bang. An errant rocket on bonfire night had hit the tarry roof of the shed where the birds were kept and exploded in a blaze of stars. The roof had been dry and newly tarred and soon was ablaze. The flames cracked the window. A passer-by saw the shed burning, opened the door and released the two birds. He called the fire brigade, and then found the birds' owner, but by then the peregrine had flown. Only the little merlin circled the shed, anxious, and came to a call. The man thought his falcon must have been burned and died, and gave up hope of finding her.

The peregrine remembered the flames. She flew far away, over the forests and woods and moors, over the hills, once taking half a rabbit that a fox had left, and tearing it hungrily. But she had not fed for days. She needed food, desperately.

She swept towards the boy, but fear mastered her and she flew up into the sky again.

Davie was no longer a prince in velvet. He was the son of a desert sheik, wearing flowing robes and jewelled belt. Behind him, waiting patiently, was his Arab mare, more beautiful than any mare in the world, her shining coat gleaming in the sun, her silken mane lying like spun glass on her proud arched neck, her flowing tail reaching to the ground, and streaming in the wind when he rode her.

He had owned her since she was born, had waited with his father the sheik the long night through, while the wind flickered over the desert sand and the bright stars watched and the women slept. Horses were men's business. He had helped to dry the foal, massaged the long slender legs, had helped her stand and suck. Such a foal, his father had said softly. Never has there been such a foal. She will be swifter than the speeding hawk, will outrun every horse in the desert, will be a treasure to cherish. Guard her well, my son.

Davie had guarded her with his life. Had fed her with camel's milk to make her strong, and when she was weaned had taken the finest wheat, the fattest corn, the best oats and mixed her food himself. No one but he could catch her. No one but he could groom her. No one but he could ride her. She came to his voice and she followed him like a dog, and with her came his greyhound that was almost as fleet as she.

Her headband was jewelled. Her saddle was edged with silver and her reins were embroidered with the symbols of long life. She was an empress among the queens, ruling over all of them, and she had a spirit that matched her beauty. Should Davie's brother approach her, she kicked, and he had to dodge and run.

She cropped the grass behind him while his falcon flew against the sun. His lure was a silver lure of dove's feathers, cunningly moulded by his father's falconer to look like a dove herself. He dipped the lure so that it flew enticingly, and the bird plunged again, the din of its coming a roar on the air as its wings cut the faint cloud that shielded the sun.

Down. Down. Down.

And up again, teasing and twisting and turning, to chase a pigeon that was flying from the trees.

Davie was himself again, a boy on a lonely hill, a boy with an ache in his leg and a hunger inside him that was not all food hunger. The Arab mare cropping behind him had turned again into his father's plough mare, Queenie. She raised her head now to watch him, and he saw her brown eyes and long lashes, and knew she was as beautiful as his dream mare. She carried him over the fields when his leg was tired, and she came to him and huffed at him each morning when he first walked in the farmyard, and she came for a crust when she was not working.

She was watching the peregrine.

The pigeon fled across the sky, the falcon close behind it. A desperate winging across the mottled blue, through silken wisps of cloud and out again, over the woods. The pigeon turned sharply, jinking, and the falcon overshot and turned steeply, banking, riding high.

The pigeon was flying straight at Davie. Was racing for its life, was a frantic heartbeating terrified creature, and below it the bird noise grew to a crescendo, pealing loud, so that Davie was almost deafened.

Hawk! Hawk! Hawk!

Blackbird and starling, thrush and lark, the loud yell of a cock pheasant, the scream of a jay, all combined together to echo the panic of the fleeing pigeon.

The bird was over the farmyard. It jinked again, turning sharply, and vanished through a hole in the barn roof. Baulked, the peregrine climbed the sky, circling, wide wings sweeping effortlessly, and the bird noise softened.

Davie drew a long pent breath, and waved his scarf again.

The falcon was exhausted.

She saw the boy and saw the swinging fringe on the scarf and flew down, landing with a thump on Davie's shoulder, gripping the thick stuff of his coat with fierce talons.

'*Aieeeee*. Gently, gently,' Davie said softly, and turned his head to meet the ringed brown and yellow eye. He remembered that birds do not like being stared at, and looked beyond her. She nibbled his ear with a gentle beak, expecting food. Davie had one sandwich left. He broke the bread, but the bird wanted meat.

Davie held a slice of beef in his fingers. The bird took it in her talons, and dipped her head and tore. She stood to swallow and dipped again. Davie held his breath lest he frighten her away.

The falcon was belled and there were leather jesses on her legs. Davie had a length of strong nylon string in his pocket, and threaded it through the rings at the ends of the jesses and held it firm. His falcon was tethered.

He was the king's son, owning a peregrine. He was the sheik's son. He would take the bird home and find her jewelled hood, the tiny leather helmet that blinded the bird and shut out fear. His matched his falcon's name and was truly splendid; tooled with gold and covered in tiny gems that glittered more brightly than the noonday sun. Diamond and ruby. Pearl and emerald. And crowned by a vivid plume of dyed bird's feathers, nodding like the plume on a knight's helmet, scarlet and yellow, azure and white.

Davie rubbed a finger along the soft creamy breast. The

falcon was still hungry, but she knew she was caught. She was a female, a large bird, and had always loved man. She waited dreamily, sure that food would come, and that at night she would be tethered on a safe block in a safe place, away from harm.

Behind him, a whistle sounded and the big collie came streaking from the farm gate and raced to Davie and barked at him. That meant it was time to come home. Gyp stared at the bird on Davie's shoulder, astounded. He had never seen a bird in such a place before.

Davie walked up the hill. He had forgotten his aching leg. The dog walked beside him and Queenie followed them, knowing it was stable time and feeding time, and liking human company.

Davie was prouder than a prince in velvet. He was prouder than the sheik's son. He owned a falcon. He had called it from the sky and it had come to him, obedient.

He walked into the farmyard, where his father and mother and brother were all waiting.

'Look what I've found,' he said. 'Her name is Splendour.'

'She must be lost,' his father answered. 'We must advertise and say we've found her.'

But the peregrine had come from far over the hills and her master did not see the advertisement in the local paper. No one ever answered.

Davie was the richest boy in the school when he returned. No one else owned a falcon.

Terror on the Hill

The dog fox lay, nose to tail, curled up three feet away from the stripped bones of a wild duck. There was a feather near his nose that fluttered softly as he breathed. He was wide awake, wary, every sense alert.

He lifted his head. He was a well-grown two-year-old, father of five cubs. His mate was dead now, and the cubs themselves hunting on the moor, healthy little beasts with no need of parental care.

The dog fox had come back to the earth where he had been born. He hankered for that part of the country, even though he ranged wide, foraging from Low Hill Farm to Valley Bottom, from Five Acre Field to Hangman's Hill, ranging over the moor, past the old forge and the water mill, hunting the wild duck that were his favourite food.

There were few rabbits, and the farmers were too ready with their guns for him to chance his luck round the stacks, rat hunting.

He lay now, full-grown, thick coated, his wise eyes watching, his ears pricked forward, listening, his damp nose sniff-sniffing, picking up every scent. He knew, without any need of words, that nothing moved near the opening of his den. He knew that there were birds rustling in the autumn dry leaves on the branches of the tree above him. He analysed the smells that drifted on the wind.

Smell of the hunting weasel, drifting away, as he ran far

over the hill; the nostril-prickling tang of woodsmoke from a bonfire on the farm below where the farmwife had burned her garden rubbish the night before, and the leaves were still smouldering. Earthsmell, damp from the autumn rain; the sweet smell of dying plants all around him. None of this was cause for the uneasiness that shivered through him, so that the hair of his thick rusty ruff bristled and his flanks quivered. He nerved himself, aware that he might need to run, but not yet knowing why.

It came again. A soft and faraway note, blown on the wind – the sound of the hunting horn. Behind it was the feel of thudding hooves vibrating the ground. It was that that had alarmed him. It was far away, too far for him to hear, but he could sense the earth tremor with his body, pressed flat against the telltale ground. He was fully awake at once, tensed to run.

Outside, the air was sharp with frost. The grass was rimed, the trees outlined with faery dust that glittered in the morning light. He had no eyes for this.

He had ceased to be anything but listening ears and questioning nose and wildness, ready to run. Run for his life through the woodland rides, run for his life through the moorland heather, run for his life as the sun swung across the brilliant sky, and behind him came open mouths and lolling tongues and panting breath and the thud, thud, thud of the galloping hooves, and the men who drove their horses to near exhaustion.

The hounds were out.

The hunt was up.

The red fox was at risk.

They were riding fast, the lead hound having picked up
his trail from the night before. The men were thundering
past Valley Bottom and turning west. The red fox ran
east.

Along the dry ditch where the leaves rustled a telltale,
and little mice hid in terror as he raced by, brushtail
streaming behind him. He had no eyes for them, no mind
for food, no thought of emptiness. He was running for
his life and that he knew, as well as he knew each night,
that the wild duck he hunted would fill his belly before
morning.

A boy, passing on his bicycle, saw the movement in the
bracken, heard the faraway lilting call of the hunting

horn, and pedalled on saying nothing. Let the little red fox run for ever.

East, towards the hunt, but also towards the long dry drainage pipe that would take him through the earthworks of the motorway workings, take him into the hated pipe that stank of man but that would baffle the hounds as it would mar his track. Through the pipe and down the hill and west again, west along the gully to Hangman's End, past the dying dogroses and the hedge that was twisted with Traveller's Joy, and the ditch that was stagnant and stank of foulness. Wading along through the ditch and up through the hedge again, and behind him the belling clear call of the lead hound, old Battler, who had a nose that led him unerringly, and a determination above that of any hound the Huntsman had known.

Across the new road, speeding between the cars that braked to a standstill, thinking him a dog. The Huntsman called the hounds to order ten minutes later, cursing. Foxes learned fast. This one used the traffic for his own ends. He had done it before, and now the Huntsman knew for certain they were after Red Rufus, the big dog fox he had seen hunting the duck on the pond at Beg The Question farm.

There had been floods on the meadows and the wet ground hid the scent of fox. Red Rufus floundered in the mud, but ran on gamely, aware that the trail behind him would be muted. At Seven Stacks farm he ploughed through the midden. The farmer had cleaned out the pigs and the reek of it hung on the air, chokingly. The reek of it clung to Rufus. He ran on, tongue lolling, tiring now, but behind him the sounds of the hunt died away. Even

Battler was at a loss. He hunted back along the trail, then found again and called. The Huntsman called the Hunt to order, sounding the clear notes that sent the hounds speeding, not knowing they were after a fresh fox, one of Rufus's cubs, and not the dog fox himself. The noise of the Hunt died away.

The morning was still and the dog fox rested, panting, his nose on his paws, lying in a borrowed den under the lea of the hill, savouring peace.

He slept, but did not relax his guard. One eye half-open, ears listening, absorbing the sounds around him – the sound of the cock pheasant feeding nearby and, further from him, a half-grown chick. Both were ready to fly at danger, but neither had scented fox. The wind was wrong.

There had been a badger past an hour before. The scent still clung to the tracks he had made. He was no threat. Brock went about his own business, plodding noisily through the wood, with no enemies but man. There had been mice, busy in the night about their own small affairs.

Rufus curled up more tightly. It was cold, even he knew that, in spite of the thick fur that protected him from the bitter chill of winter. His breath plumed on the air, and there was little heat in the sun's rays.

The floods had made feeding poor, drowning hare and rabbit and the fieldmice that lived in almost every hollow. Had it not been for the duck, flying in to forage in the flooded fields, the foxes would have suffered badly. As it was, Rufus was fat and contented, and lacked nothing.

There were others that lacked food. He did not rest for long. His quick ears caught the rumour of moving bodies. At once he was wide awake, head alert, listening, only his ears and his nose able to warn him of danger. He stood, head cocked, ears pricked forward, uneasiness flooding him. He did not know what threat lay waiting, but he knew that something came towards him. It was new to him and he was unprepared.

There was a rank scent and a shrill murmur.

His red ruff bristled.

His nose caught the scent, knew the scent, and knew panic. An age-old panic, inherited from ancestors long dead. He was off, running with the wind against him, flattening his fur, lips drawn back in a grinning snarl.

The weather had changed. Above him was a sulphur sky fingered with black. The sun was a brilliant disc, low on the hills. The frosted grass was a brittle sharp, rimed and grey. The stiff dead bracken bore icy fronds. The dead leaves crackled, fringed with white.

The scent of terror was borne on the wind.

Fear scent.

Horror scent.

The devil pack hunting.

Rufus had never been hunted like this before. This was worse than the clumsy men on their huge horses, audible for miles; worse than the lolloping hounds, belling noisily as they found the scent; worse than the man with a gun. Guns could be dodged.

The hunters came on, death in their minds, noses down, taking the fox scent from under the pig scent. The pack ran on crouched legs, tails stretched, the shrill shrieking from a dozen throats more terrifying than the bay of any hound.

Fear in the yellow sky.

Terror on the throbbing air.

Panic in the wind that screamed in the heather and drove the flying clouds in mounting peaks that packed as fast as the hounds packed.

The fox ran for his life.

The weasels were starving. They had found little food for days. They had come from the high moors where small life was scarce, and the hunger that drove them was wicked inside them, a burning ache that demanded instant satisfaction. They longed for blood; for the warm red meat that would give them life. They yickered as they ran.

Rusty fled on, running with the wind stroking his fur,

flattening his ears, thrusting through his brush. This time he made for the high ground, flying up the hill with the wind at his heels, passing Nine Men's Groaning and High Peak Hollow, up the Seven Beeches hill towards Hanging Ditch and Heystones. Fear stalked behind him.

The hunters sped on.

No use running into cover; cover was betrayal. No use diving into shelter. The weasels could follow. No use climbing above them. No use swimming. Nothing would deter them. Nothing would shake them. Nothing would halt them.

He was panic racing on four legs. He was knotted fear in his heart and tenseness in his belly. He was losing ground and losing breath and the following wind brought the smell of death towards him. Fear smell, terror smell, little hunters raging at his heels. A quick snap and he leaped forward again, panic giving him strength.

Above him the yellow sky brooded and blackened.

Flame spat from the clouds. Flame crackled and thunder rolled. A ball of fire dropped from the heavens and hit a tree that split with a mighty crack. The weasels ran on. They were close, and the scent of fox was enticement, was food smell in their nostrils, was the answer to hunger, and nothing would deter them.

The fox hesitated as the thunder rolled again, rolling over the hills, echoing from the peaks, rumbling distantly to die in a soft groan as the first weasel sprang.

Teeth closed.

They met nothing but fur.

The fox twisted in his tracks, snapped twice, and the weasel fell, broken backed.

There was a brief respite.

The ravening pack turned cannibal and stopped to feed. They fed fast and there were many of them.

The fox crossed water, confusing his track, but his scent hung nose high and was rank on the air, and the pack came on, red-eyed, relentless. He made better eating than one small weasel, shared between twenty.

High on the hill was a wood, a maze of trees, uncleared by man. It was thick with coppice, and he raced among the tangle, confusing his trail, leaping dead branches, diving under bramble, but the pack came on still. They were small and lithe and where he led they could follow.

Death was a heartbeat away.

The wood was doubtful sanctuary. He left it for the open moor, running in circles, dodging like an old hare to avoid the racing hound, leaping sideways, returning on his track, but the killers came on, undeterred.

Thunder rolled around them. Rain fell, briefly, soaking the ground, soaking the fur of hunter and hunted alike, but the hunt was up and the blood lust was fiercer than any fear of the weather, and victory was in sight.

Another weasel sprang. The fox leaped out of range and raced downhill, through wet bracken that masked his vision, through the bog patch where the yellow moss was spongy underfoot and his paws splashed clumsily, slowing his pace.

The weasels followed.

On to solid ground again, round the margin of a lake where the duck caught the scent of fear and took flight, wings drumming, powerful bodies surging through the air.

Thunder rolled all round them.

Lightning seared from the clouds, spearing towards the ground, flashing in sheets again and again and again. It hit the roof of the tithe barn at Seven Hills End, and the hay blazed, and the men raced, bringing hoses. It struck the steeple of the church at Nether Willow, knocking off the cross from the top. It struck a house in Willow Martin and killed a cow at Upper Lancing.

The fox ran on.

He had forgotten safety. He knew only fear. Fear of the ravening creatures behind him, fear of death in the sodden heather, fear of unknown darkness, of teeth tearing at him, of the end of all he knew. He had no knowledge but that of his own hunting. He knew the running beast and he knew the sudden cease of life at the kill. He knew the tear of savage teeth.

Afternoon had gone and darkness had come to the wilderness. On the far horizon man's lights patched the gloom. On the road headlights arched and scythed the sky. Beyond them was the orange glow of a big city, an un-dreamed of place beyond the knowledge of the running beasts.

Rufus turned towards the road. Cars helped him foil the hunt. They might help him foil the weasel pack. He was tiring fast. He had run far and fast from the hounds, and had not rested long before he ran again. He padded wearily, brush held low. He was almost defeated. The breath was raw in his throat. He lifted his head and snarled at a hunting owl as it swooped low. It dived behind him and rose again, with one of the smallest weasels held in its talons. One hunter less. The pack was undeterred. The fox looked back over his shoulder. Angry eyes gleamed, firepoints in the dusk.

He came at last to the road. He dived across and into the ditch at the far side. A headlight etched him briefly against the dark, and then he was gone, a memory only in a man's surprised mind as he cruised home after a week spent away working in a distant town. His thoughts were on his family, on his supper, and he noted the fox and stored the memory to tell the children when he saw them in the morning.

The fox ran on.

The weasels followed. They had never known roads.

The survivors were undeterred.

Starvation was master.

They were failing too, but not so fast as the fox. He came to a field and ran down the furrow, the straw stubble cutting his paws. He could not go on. He had no strength left. He longed for rest. Longed for the deep and silent dark, far underground, but there was no safety there.

He ran through the hedge and came to a farmyard where light spilled through an open doorway. Light was an enemy. He ran through the shadows, away from the danger, his paws sounding doglike on the cobbles. The farm dog barked, a welkin baying that roared in the silence. The farmer shouted and ran into the yard.

The fox saw blackness, saw safety, saw sanctuary, and raced inside. The farmworker, passing, saw the open door and cursed and slammed it shut. The farmer saw the weasel pack and yelled to his wife to bring the gun, thinking that this was what had alerted the dog, thinking of his hens and his cattle and the ravening beasts.

The gun wrought terror and the weasels ran. They narrowly missed the striped tabby cat that sprang to a wall and hissed defiance. Within a moment, faster than smokehaze drifting over the stubble, they were gone.

The fox skirted the stable uneasily. It stank of horse. He was too tired to care and the horse did not threaten him. It stared at him, uneasy. But old Blackie was used to fox smell. Two cubs played regularly in the field where he spent the summer. He bent his head to his haynet and began to crop. Rufus curled in the straw of the manager and went to sleep.

No one saw him.

When the old horse was led out to graze in the field the fox left his warm bed and went out into the morning. The farm was large. There were barns throughout the fields. Barns filled with hay to feed the winter cattle. Barns where a fox could hide for ever and not be seen.

The fox made a den in the hay. It was warm, and the winter wind was kept at bay, and he fed on rat and mouse and vole. One morning, one of the boys who lived on the farm watched him hunting and told his father.

'Cheeky devil,' the farmer said. His hens were well protected and they had no ducks or geese, and the fox was keeping the vermin down as efficiently as the farmyard cats. Let him stay.

By the end of the winter he was not only a familiar sight, but he was tame and touchable, coming like a dog when one of the boys called him. He came for bones which they spread out on the lawn. Visitors were surprised to see the red-coated shape slip out of the barn and cross the field and stand, regal, in front of the house, looking fearlessly at the faces in the window.

No one dared hunt him that winter.

He sheltered through all the time of ice and frost and snow. He fed fat. He was tolerated by the dogs.

And then came spring and a morning of bright sunshine and light sparkling on the tiny curled leaves of new growing heather, and a March hare madness everywhere. There was a scent on the air; the calling enticement of a vixen over the hill.

When the boys next looked in the barn, the fox had gone.

The Outcast

THE OUTCAST

This is the story of a rare creature—a hummel—a stag that never grows antlers. He can become more ferocious than any antlered stag and fight his way into acceptance by the herd. And his sons grow antlers, like any other stag. No one knows why it happens.

The leader of the stag herd was dead. His successor gloried and took the old lord's harem. Twelve gentle little hinds followed him wherever he went, and with them came their calves, small and playful, dancing and butting in mock battle in the thick heather.

The old leader had been deposed two years before, but one hind stayed faithful to him. One old hind, grey muzzled, followed him in the rutting season and eased his loneliness. He was ageworn and weary and his once proud antlers were no longer handsome. They were poor adornments that showed his years. His muzzle was grey and he could no longer run, or fight to hold his place. Even his roars were feeble, mockeries of the savage exultancies all around him.

The old Hill Master was dead, but the hind would bear his son this season. She too was old and it would be the last calf she would nurse.

She rested through the winter months, conserving her strength. Age had given her wisdom. She grazed with the

younger hinds and helped to guard them, warning them
of the running fox, and the eagle, whose shadow raced
across the hill terrifying all of them for he took their
calves. She warned them too of man scent, borne on the
wind, as the hunters came stalking with their guns.

She knew where the moss grew juiciest. She knew
where the grazing was untouched by harsh winter. She
knew where the villagers stored their turnips, and which
shed would open at the touch of her thrusting nose. She
knew which fields were unguarded and she knew where
the keeper threw the winter hay for the ponies, and was
the first to find it.

Her baby was strong when he was born, and she had

plenty of milk for him. He thrived, and was heavier than the other staggie calves born that year, and stronger. He was taller, and could butt and kick with the best of them, pushing with his hard little forehead until his opponent was forced to give way.

There were games on the hill all summer long, as the little calves chased and butted and fought, struggling to see which was master. They raced against each other, strengthening muscles that they needed for running fast and fleet. They could not fight their enemies, but depended on the quickness of their speeding hooves. Only, sometimes, when faced by terror, the hinds turned to kick, and several shecats had broken ribs to show where they had tangled with an enraged mother, ardent in defending her young.

Now came another winter. This time the old hind had no calf to cheer her and she stayed with her lastborn. Together she showed him where the grazing was good and took him to the turnip fields, and led him to the barns where there was hay to tug and steal from the horses. The farmers knew when the deer had been by and cursed, but they never caught them. They only saw the tracks of their tiny neat hooves in the mud and the toss and tumble where they had dragged the hay from the ricks, feeding in the dawnlight when man lay sleeping inside his shuttered home.

Spring came and flowers starred the hillside and glowed in the undergrowth in the dark dank woods. There was spring grass and new green shoots on the heather and the tight-furled leaves of bracken. The deer went north. The yearling stags were strong now. The first buds of new antlers thrust from their foreheads, covered in dark velvet that was rich with stored blood. Inside the velvet the growing horn itched and ached like a newborn tooth. The stags were irritable and left the herd to browse alone, often father and son together or half-brother with half-brother, standing guard while one fed; using double vigilance to escape from the sounding guns that were their only danger now they were grown. Men came to poach on the hill, evading the keeper, knowing there was a good price for venison in the city hotels, and cooks did not ask questions.

The old hind waited for her son to start his growing pains. She had borne seven sons and four daughters, and she knew well that soon he would leave her and go off into the distant glens. But her son remained equable. His temper never changed. He was content to graze with her, and did not understand why his fellow stags had left him, nor did he understand the new hard knobs on their heads, or why they lashed out at him in genuine fury if he tried the old game of butt and push.

Summer passed, but his forehead was as unmarked as any hind's. The stags returned to the hinds, bearing new antlers proudly. They roared their challenges, heads lowered, antlers lying along their backs, turning to north, to south, to east, to west, until the hill was noisy with their urgent bellowing, with their constant voices lifted in anger, as they took the hinds and held them against other stags and ran, collie-wise, round and round, trying to keep any one from escaping. They grew thin, as there was never time to feed. Life was constant vigilance and constant wariness.

The young stags were driven out. The older stags were fierce and powerful, and would not tolerate the youngsters. The old hind's lastborn watched in puzzlement. He had no such growths on his head. Nor could he fight the older deer. Those antlers could rake and hurt, as he soon discovered.

He left the herd and left his mother, and went to the hilltop, alone and outcast, unable to understand why he was different. The hinds ignored him.

His mother had taught him well. He knew where to find the best food. He knew where to look for the most succulent mosses. He knew, when winter lashed the hills with frenzy, where to find shelter from the gales, where to find hay, and where to find turnips. He knew where there was a deserted field that once housed a pony, and he took the open shelter for his own. The children sometimes saw him there when the weather was bad and thought he was a hind, as he bore no antlers.

When spring came, his forehead was still smooth. The stags were angry again, guarding the aching knobs with care, avoiding all challenge. Now the stag knew he was different. Men who saw him realized now he was grown that he was a rarity, a hummel, but his heavy body and thick ruff and powerful shoulders showed that he was a male and no timid hind. He was already larger than any stag born in his year.

He matched his strength against the trees. A forester watched in amazement one day as he saw the hummel straining against a young pine, not resting until he had pushed it to the ground, leaving it with roots half exposed to the air. The man replanted it after the stag had gone, and spoke of the antlerless beast on the hill, challenging the forest as he could not challenge his own kind.

Three summers passed.

The hummel was lonely. He returned to the herd, following at a distance. The stags grazed near one another, ignoring one another. The hinds and the newborn calves and last year's young all grazed together lower down the hillside. The old hind was now the grandmother of all the herd, the veteran, and it was she who warned them of danger, she who guarded the little ones while their mothers fed or rested, she whose voice sounded often, barking sharply to tell of man or soaring eagle or chasing fox. She was waywise and knew more than any of them.

That year, in the rutting time, when the stags were gathering the hinds, the hummel stood on a pinnacle on the rock and bayed defiance.

The other stags stared at him.

A stranger.

Without antlers.

Contemptuous, they continued to fight one another, and ignored the hummel.

Angered, he surveyed the hinds. Among them was one that was slender and delicate, her small head lifted to look at him, wide brown eyes appealing. He went to her and nosed her gently, pushing her out of the herd, coaxing her to come with him, to follow him. She stared up at him, her nostrils quivering. He was strong and male and exciting, and she turned and went with him, deserting her own mate.

The stag she had left behind ran after her, bellowing his rage. The hummel lashed at him with his hooves,

catching his challenger in the ribs with such force that he overbalanced and fell. The victor walked towards the herd and nudged out another hind. She followed too, and the two hinds watched as the second deserted stag roared furious challenge.

The hummel had no time to turn. He braced himself for the onrush as the stag came at him, antlers lowered, ready to thrust at neck and chest. Feet apart, the challenger waited, stock-still, and neatly inserted his bare head between the pointed spikes.

Then he braced his forelegs and shoulders and pushed with all his might. The antlered stag, shaken by the shock of impact, was unready. He was forced backwards, breathing hard. He ended with his rump pressed against a tree, unable to move farther, and tried to rally.

But the hummel was too quick. Long hours spent strengthening his head and shoulders were giving him his reward now. He leaped away and boxed at the stag, who raised himself and boxed back. But a double kick landed and once more the hummel was victor. The loser went back to his other hinds, his ribs bruised and aching.

The hummel rounded up three more hinds, leaving one young stag to spend the autumn in angry bachelorhood. The hummel was confident now. He saw the leader of the herd, a great stag with huge antlers, lordly and supreme. He was massive and powerful and, as the antlerless stag came up to him, looked down.

The Hill Master had not dreamed that he would be challenged. He was quite unprepared for the head that butted him between his wide-spreading crown. He thrust, but the head did not move, and there was no way of out-manoeuvring so that he could free his own weapons and use them in battle.

The hummel pushed. The Hill Master was strong, but no normal beast had such strength as this unnatural creature from the forest, fighting by unknown means, using enormous strength to defeat any that dared defy him.

Inch by slow, reluctant inch, the great stag retreated.

The cliff ended in a long grassy slope. Rain had fallen for days and the ground was treacherous. The stag tried to change his position, but he had no chance. His relentless enemy followed every step, every shift pushing the Hill Master closer to the edge.

The last few feet were easy. The grass gave impetus to

the hummel's slow thrust. He pushed with all his strength, and the Hill Master lost his footing and slid downwards, his heavy body unable to brake. He fell onto gravel, and took the hill with him as he came to the scree and started an avalanche that tore away part of the mountain. Bruised, defeated and shaken, the old Hill Master did not return the challenge.

The hummel took the leader's harem. He climbed to the best grazing place. He stood on the naked rock and shouted his triumph in a mighty roar.

Next year the young calves were larger and stronger than any before as the hummel's sons and daughters saw the light of day. All the males grew fine strong antlers, and no more hummels were born on the hill. But it was years before there was a new Hill Master. The hummel reigned supreme.

Storm

STORM

The storm wind from the Atlantic came raging from the sky. Storm crash of surf thundered on the beaches. The screaming gale raced among the dark ragged cloud packs and whipped them to a frenzy. Rain lashed in torrents on the wild white tasselled waves. Spray was flung in towering fountains as the sea fought the grim spikes of rocks.

Boats fled to shelter. Men ran for cover. The seagulls flew inland to the fields and furrows, where the wind was not so fierce. Foxes hid underground, badgers curled nose to tail and little mice dived into holes. Beast and bird were soaked with rain, but most found shelter.

Only on the driven beaches, where the boulders rolled in the wind and the sea clawed at the cliffs, the mother seals could find no protection. The big bulls were safe at sea. Here they stayed until the turmoil had died.

But the babies were almost newborn, too young to swim and could not be left. The mothers were frantic. Some had taken their young to the shelter of caves, but there were too many seals on the beaches for all to find comfort.

There were forty seals lying against the wall of cliff, while the sea fought to tear their babies from them. The mothers had turned their bodies to challenge the water. The little ones were shielded from the angry grabbing waves, that flew up the shingle with a suck and a swirl and a seethe and smashed against the rocks in a wildness of white water.

There was noise everywhere. The roar of the wind and the fierce growl of the water, and the rumble of rocks, tossed by fury, so that the seals were battered and bruised and terrified. They had never known such weather. Many of them were young and these were their first calves, but they guarded them as well as the older seals, and watched the wise mothers and learned from them.

Take the brunt of the sea, and protect the younglings. Nuzzle and nurse and gentle the panic. The babies cried, but only their mothers heard them. This was terror beyond a seal's imagining, this crescendo of noise, of wind-lashed water, of rain so hard that it hurt and, then, of hailstones, bigger than marbles, beating out of the air, striking defenceless heads, bouncing off the rocks and striking again on a ricochet.

Bruise and beat and batter, until the mother seals were crying too, were raising their voices in frenzy, not knowing how to bear the misery, afraid that the sea would tear their babies from them as it had torn one of the smallest only a short hour ago.

The mother had turned briefly, weary of punishment, to ease her eyes from the wind's sting, and in that moment a giant wave leaped in and siezed the tiny seal calf and carried it seawards. The mother had plunged into the waves, but the rocks defeated her. The baby drowned.

She dragged herself from the water and roamed the beach, seeking, seeking, and as she passed the mothers who still kept their babies, she snarled her misery and snapped at their faces, and they crouched closer, guarding

the little ones, desperate to ensure that they survived.

There was one seal at the end of the beach who was wiser than her sisters. Her baby was so new that he was barely four hours old, and her instincts taught her that he must be shielded from the weather or he might not live. Instinct drove her to take him in her jaws.

Instinct drove her along the edge of the cliff, pressed close against the rock, stopping when the waves crashed, holding him in her teeth. He was warm and alive and she loved him more than she loved life itself, and determination taught her what she must do. She gripped him so tightly that he whimpered softly, but she dared not let go. The sea would take him.

She pulled herself over a rock, fighting the wind that tore at her head. She was a slender little seal, only just full grown herself, and her doglike head was graced by deep brown eyes that glowed when she looked at the little soft calf that clung from her jaws.

He was heavy, and she had to rest. She had to watch the sea. She had to turn so that he was out of reach of the waves, held by her body against the cliff. She had to brace herself as the water rolled her. She had to watch as she climbed lest the sea seize them both. She had to remember the path she had found long ago, when she was young, and busy exploring the strange world in which she found herself.

A wild world of wind and water, with little protection from the weather, with the smell of seaweed ever in her nostrils, but with hidden tunnels in the cliffs that offered sanctuary. One of these, in particular, she remembered. It had been some distance above the beach and difficult of access, especially for a creature that could only drag herself along. In the water she could fly like a bird through the waves, swimming swiftly, turning fleetly, diving cleanly, but here she was hampered by her bulk and by her lack of running legs.

She paused behind a rock, briefly out of the wind, to catch her breath. She put her baby down gently and stood above him, ready to grab him should the sea reach towards here. As yet, this rock was dry. Only the hail beat down on the cliff above her and lashed the overhang that protected her from the wind's whip and the rain's lances.

The next wave spilled over the rock and edged towards her. It was time to go. Time to lift the little one, so that he hung helpless, time to push out of shelter and into the din and surge and rumble, to feel the spray as it flashed skywards and fell back again, to feel the rain on her back and head, to be deafened by the din and torment.

The rocks were slippery and the seaweed hampered her progress. There were sharp barnacles that tore at her dense fur and at her pads and tail. She held the baby high. He was little and vulnerable. She crept on, feeling the sea come nearer at each step. The wind screamed round the crannies. A rock fell from above and was fragmented. A sharp corner tore at her head, and blood dripped into one eye. She shook her head, defying the world about her.

Through a crack in the cliffs, and up over the rocks again, now out of reach of the greedy sea but in danger of falling. Darkness had come and the world was a nightmare of wind and roaring water, and she was forced to fight every inch of the way, to hunt for the opening she knew was there.

She found it at last.

She was inside the crack and was safe, out of the rain and out of the wind. She dropped her baby in the sand.

There had never been a storm like this in all the history of the island. The raging wind had built the sea to such heights that it came where it had never come before, and even as the seal rested the first suck of water spilled into her hiding-place. She grabbed her baby and fled into the crack, knowing that it climbed, knowing that it was wide enough to let her pass, knowing that it ended in a high cave that led to the grassy top of the island.

She did not know that halfway up the passage the cliff had slipped and the way was almost blocked.

She came to the blockage.

Behind her, the sea reached for her tail, and she knew that she was trapped.

She had to save her baby.

Every instinct in her body drove her. She nosed the fall of rock. The stones were loose.

She laid the baby against the fall, holding it with her body, guarding it from harm from the sea and from any rock that might slip, shielding it with her head, and she began to work.

Slowly and carefully, she pushed the topmost rock of the fall. It was wedged, but not too tightly. And she was heavy. She thrust with every muscle and the rock slipped away, leaving a gap, not yet large enough to let her force her way but large enough for her to work.

There were other smaller stones which she took in her her jaws and laid on the ground beside her, careful to see that they did not slip and crush her youngling. The little seal nosed her, hungry, wanting to feed, but she had no time and she touched him with her nose, warning him, telling him in the only way she knew that he must lie still.

The sea reached in and soaked her tail and hind flippers. If she did not hurry they would both be trapped. The raging waves would tear her baby from her. It would throw her against the rocky sides, seethe through the gap she had made and send the boulders flying, and they would be caught in an inferno. She knew none of this. She only knew there was danger. Danger! Every instinct shouted to her to hurry, hurry, hurry.

She pulled the rocks and pushed the rocks. She thrust

the rocks aside. She nosed her way through, but the gap
was not yet large enough, and if she put the baby through
alone and could not follow he would die. This too she
knew without need of thought. He had to stay with her.
He needed milk and her warmth and care. He needed her
to guard him against other seals. He needed her to guard
him against the wild toss of the sea.

Incautiously, spurred on by haste as the sea crept forward and sucked at her with a rage and a roar, she pulled
at one of the lower rocks and it slipped. Those above it
crashed around her, terrifying her with the echo of the din.
One fell against her unwounded eye and blood poured
from yet another small cut. But the gap in the blockage
was larger.

Now she worked more carefully, holding each small
rock tight in her jaws, building another wall behind her.
If the sea came through, she would soon be doubly
trapped. Another wave licked past, lapping at her fur.

Another rock. And another.

Behind her was the wild scream of the wind as it tore
along the cliffs, the terrifying cry of seagulls, flying inland,
away from the water, and the roar, in the lulls, of the
other seals as they strove to keep their babies out of reach
of the waves. By now five little ones had been flung to
die against the sharp teeth of the rocks and five mothers
were mourning, hunting along the sea's edge, and being
thrown by the waves.

Another rock shifted and the gap was large enough for
her to lift her baby in her jaws and force her body through.
The sea tore after her, tumbling the rocks she had moved,
bellowing in the narrow opening, but now she was on sand

again, and the way led upwards. She ran as fast as a seal could run on her clumsy flippers. Only in the sea was she swift and beautiful.

Upwards, over soft sand into which her flippers dug deep, upwards, dragging her heavy body along, leaving gouges that marked her trail. Upwards, with the sea reaching in towards her, seeking to drag her back, soaking sand that had lain unmarked for years, tearing at the rocks that she had moved, sliding them backwards and forwards, tumbling them, playing with them, tossing them, until they were spread along the passage, leaving the way clear for the next wave to fly after her and soak her to the shoulders.

Upwards. With the baby hanging heavy in her jaws, afraid of the din and the turmoil and the wild screeches in the narrow caveways. Upwards, pausing to breathe, pausing to lay the little one down and rest aching jaws and weary muscles. She was not yet recovered from the exhaustion of birth. The storm had been raging for three days, growing in ferocity, the wind a racing demon shouting along the cliffs, tearing great branches from the landlorn trees, flinging giant trunks groundwards, snatching roots, that had stood for centuries, out of the reluctant earth, pushing with all its might against the woods that withstood it.

The wind was fear. The wind was terror. The wind was an invisible creature, riding the air, hunting the clouds, packing the grey masses thick in the wild sky. The wind was always there, on the desolate winter beaches, on the ravaged cliffs, where the trees were few and stunted and dwarfed and pointed to the land, their branches perpetually stroked away from the sea. But never a wind like this.

Upwards and on.

There was a lull in the wind, a pause in the sounds, a release from the sea. The sand was dry again. But the wind was now in her face again and, when it started to blow, the sand blew back in the mother seal's eyes, stinging and blinding, so that she closed her lids and blundered on, aware only of pain.

Pain in her sandfilled eyes. Pain from the cuts on her head. Pain from flippers that were torn and bleeding where she had fought the rockfall. Pain from the aching jaw muscles that had held her son for so long.

The tunnel opened.

She was on the cliff top. There was light again, a little light from an angry sky that was as tumbled as the water. Clouds raged across a moon that was almost hidden. Clouds built on the horizon. Clouds that hung heavy and threatening, filled with more rain.

She dragged herself out of the cave mouth, afraid that the sea might rage after her, not knowing that it could never climb so high. She had to go on, on and up. The little island was pointed, crowned by thorn trees, under which was a mossy hollow. Here she had climbed to sunbathe on hot summer afternoons long, long ago, before winter froze the land.

There was little cover from the thorn. The branches were bare, and rain hung in shivering drops from every twig. She crept beneath them, and the hummock hid her from the wind that whipped icily across its top. She was out of breath and exhausted.

She dropped her baby on the wet moss. He crawled to push against her, hungry to nurse, seeking the milk that he needed so badly. It was a long time since he had fed.

He sucked noisily, and she nosed his small head, and watched the wind rip the clouds to long ragged streamers, edged with brilliant light. The moon silvered the ground. The moon shone on the flurry in the waters, shone on the crowded beaches where the other seals still battled against the suck and swirl of the tide.

She slept and her baby slept beside her, warm and safe and comforted, both of them exhausted by the long struggle upwards from the terrible stormswept beach.

The wind fell out of the night. The waves dropped with the receding tide and fingered the rocks tenderly, smoothing past. The seal mothers below nursed their young, and the sun came clear out of a sharp blue sky and warmed the colony. Far above them, out of danger, the small seal woke and played with a feather, and his mother watched him and groaned with pleasure.

The storm was over.

Shadows on the Hillside

The wildcat laired on one of the most inaccessible mountains in that part of Scotland.

From her den she could see the wild sweep of pines that spanned the hillside and met the loch. She could see the town that nestled under the shoulder of the lowest peak and the patched lights that sprang to mark it every night. She could see the slash and swathe of headlights as cars sped past on the road far below.

She never ventured into the realms of men.

Her home was the wide hill and the racing burn, the bleak moor where small mice hid beneath the sparse clumps of heather, and small birds flew from the wind-swept trees, and the mountain hare bounded at dusk and at the dawning.

Her knowledge was of the windy sky, and the scents that called her, lying on the ground, telling of food, telling of hunting and telling of the tomcat that was seeking her for his springtime mating.

He came and stayed for a week and was gone again, and she grew heavy with kits. They were her first kits and she did not yet know the ways of motherhood. Her own mother had drowned in a winter flood, and she had never seen kittens before.

She did not need anything but the instincts that taught her to hunt, to gather strength and to find a safe place in which to lie. She wanted shelter. Shelter from the ever-present wind that keened above the heather, shelter from the terrible rainstorms that lashed out of a troubled sky, shelter from the cold.

She found a tiny cave above the burn that dropped, a few yards from her, into a pool far below. The noise of water was always in her ears.

She was young and not yet wise.

She bore her litter one windy night in May. By morning four kittens cuddled close against her flanks. She brooded over them, her eyes glowing with pride. Nothing in the world had ever meant so much as this. Her loud purr comforted the tiny creatures, as they lay against her warm body and sucked life from her teats.

She was a tabby cat, her fur bushy, her ringed short tail clublike and immense. Her ears stood sideways on her flattened head, and when anger roused her she was the embodiment of hate, a spitting fury that no other creature dared challenge.

She was shy of man and ran from him whenever he came near. She only wanted to be left in peace, to live her life on the wide hillside and rear her kits. She licked them gently and nosed each tiny head that nuzzled blindly. They were very small.

Eight days passed. She hunted near to her den, feeding swiftly, afraid of the other creatures that fed on the hill. Afraid of the slinking stoat and the wily weasel, cunning enough to follow her trail, cunning enough to find her lair, and hungry enough to take her young and leave her desolate.

During the eighth night rain began to fall on the hills.

At first it was only a murmur, a soft patter of thin drops falling from a grey sky. The clouds built, until there were massive rolling bulks of darkness, and the rain came with night, in torrents. Sleet and snow followed in quick succession and then rain again.

The burn filled.

When morning came the little cat stepped out into a world of terror. The hillside was a rolling mass of water, and she herself was only just above the rising burn. Her cave would soon be flooded.

She had to save her kittens.

She seized the first, a little heavy tom, in her jaws, and bounded up the hill, away from the intrusive water, over

123

the rocks, over the shale, over the scree, on and up. Up till she was within sight of the eagle himself, and here was more danger.

He too was hungry.

He too had young.

There was an old burrow under a rock. The cat dug fiercely, dug swiftly, dug deep. She dropped the kitten inside, and fled downwards, her paws slipping as she ran. Time was against her and she was afraid of the rising water, afraid that the kittens would vanish. Fear lent her strength. She knew without need of words or thoughts that here was danger. She had fallen in water herself and hated it, although she had swum to safety.

Above her, the eagle circled, watching to see where she hid her young.

They were still too small to run. They could not yet see. She lifted the second in her mouth, a tiny female who mewed piteously when she was lifted from the warm nest where she had lain close against her brother and sister.

There was no time to stop. The cat ran up the hill, over the rocks and over the scree, but now she was slower, she was tiring. The kitten was heavy and the way was long, and the eagle watched her and she was afraid. She did not know that he was wary of her fierce claws and teeth. He had met other wildcats on the hill.

Once she slipped and rolled downwards, scratching desperately at the ground, trying to brake her speed, but she never once opened her mouth or let the kitten go. She had to hurry, to race against the water and bring the kits to safety. Their life was all important. For this, she was born.

She laid the little one in the burrow beside her brother.

The tomcat tried to suck his sister's ear, and was disappointed. He was hungry. He snuggled against her. He had been cold and lonely by himself. She was comfort and she was company and his mother was near. The wildcat nosed them both before she left them.

Down the hill, over the scree and over the rocks, now slippery and treacherous. Rain was falling again to add to her discomfort and the wind was blowing in her face. She hated wind and she hated the rain that soaked her coat. She reached the den.

The water had risen. It lapped gently, only a few inches below the opening of the cave. It threshed over the rocks and fell with an almighty roar that deafened the cat and terrified her even more. She grabbed the second little tom and left his sister alone, and sped again up the hill, driving herself to hurry, racing along, though the breath pulled in her throat and her small heart was pounding, and fear dominated every other feeling.

The way was even longer than before. Uphill, pushing against the slimy rocks and the sodden ground. Uphill, knowing the eagle was watching. Uphill, with the wind behind her and the little kit a weight in her jaws, and the mountain fighting her, every inch of the way.

Uphill, and the den was reached at last and the third kitten laid in safety, to wriggle and settle against the other two, while the mother, this time, did no more than drop it fast and run again.

Run, fighting the wind and the rain and the wicked muddy ground, down which she slipped and slithered. Run, to find the water lapping at the door of the cave and the last kitten lying in a small pool. Snatch the kitten and race outside, and then legs and tail were caught by the flood and the cat was in the burn, and the kitten was under water.

She snatched at the bank with tearing claws. There was a tree trunk leaning perilously over the stream, and she caught the bark and pulled herself out. She was saturated and exhausted. She had little energy left. But the kitten was alive and safe, moving her small paws and head, and mewing her discomfort.

The wildcat rested on the sloping tree trunk. There was water beneath her, but it had not yet surrounded her. She waited, and then she ran up the tree and dropped to dry ground, only a few feet above the encroaching flood.

This time she could not hurry. She was bruised and battered and sore. She dragged herself slowly up the scree and over the rocks, and inch by inch up the mountainside, aware only of exhaustion, of rain falling in torrents, of wind screaming behind her.

Lightning flashed on the hills.

She had never seen lightning before. She ran, hurrying to reach her other babies, hurrying to hide from the blinding flash, hurrying ever faster as thunder pealed and echoed and rolled, and the terrible mountains shouted their anger at her.

She reached the burrow at last. She dropped the fourth kitten inside and tried to follow. The opening was too narrow. It would not let her in. Only her head could follow her kittens now.

She nosed them unhappily. She was too tired to dig. She lay across the entrance, guarding them with her body. She could not warm them. She could not creep out of the rain and the wind. She could not find comfort.

She lay through the night, while the rain ceased and the moon arose and silvered the land about her. Dawn came, with a warm sun that gave her strength.

One by one, she lifted the kittens into the open air, and lay with them and licked their soft heads and let them suck. Above her the eagle circled endlessly, watching. If one should stray . . .

The eagle saw a hare, dived and killed. The cat was safe for that day. There was food and to spare for his young, but she did not know she was safe. She only knew that the eagle laired above her and she must find sanctuary.

He had gone from the sky. She basked in the warmth,

feeling the heat dry her fur, seeing her kittens stumble and roll and play, uneasy on their legs, but today, for the first time, their eyes were open. They stared about them, and she knew instinctively that she must hide them from the midday sun.

The wildcat looked about her. She was high on the windy hill. When rain dulled the land and dimmed the sky the tenuous clouds would cover her home. But now there was sun and the midday blaze and clear blue sky above her. She basked for an hour, while the kittens revelled in unfamiliar sunshine. She fed the little ones and cuddled them close. Her rich purr startled a stag as he came towards her, and fled. She did not see or scent him.

There was a crack in the rocks, wide and deep, and shadowed. The wildcat left her kittens, first dropping them safely into the hole she had dug—the hole that would not allow her to enter.

It was dark and cold in the crack. It was hidden and shadowed. But there was a tree growing out of the rock and a deep cave beneath it, filled with dead leaves. Here she could curl in safety. Here she could hide the kittens from sight. From here they could run down the hill and play in the sunlight and she could watch over them.

It would be days before they could climb out alone.

She returned to the hole and moved the kittens, one by one. The crack was chilly after the warm air outside, but the leaves were dry and soft, and some other creature had denned there before her and made the bed snug with sheep's wool, gathered from the heather.

The cat curled against her kittens, her head across their small bodies. She licked them clean. She cherished them and, when they were older, she taught them how to hunt and how to kill.

She taught them well, so that when the shadow of the eagle fled across the hill they crouched in the heather, still as the stones that lay on the mountainside, and the bird saw nothing.

When winter came, five wildcats hunted on the hill. They played in the snow, and kept the farms beneath them free from rats, and no man saw them.

Fire in the Forest

FIRE IN THE FOREST

The four boys had been walking all morning. It was time
to eat. Malcolm was to gather the sticks, Davie was to
fetch the water, Roger was to tend the fire and Paul would
cook.

They looked about them. The serried mass of pines
dropped away to the distant loch. It was very peaceful and
very quiet. No one else existed.

The only sound was the wind that gathered in the trees,
and sped round the heavy trunks, brushing the stiff
branches. It had not rained for weeks and everywhere was
dry.

So dry that Davie had to walk half a mile before
he found a pool in the burn with enough water to fill
the can. So dry that when Roger lit the fire the sparks
flew on the air and caught the branch of a tree above
him.

So dry that he could not beat the flames out. They
spread and danced, and the little red specks of fire flew
along the branches—and the boys ran. Ran to find the
forest ranger and confess their crime. There were homes
in the forest. There were beasts in the forest, and they had
not known that fire could fly so fast.

The flames flew on the racing wind that was strengthening every minute. The wind had been biding its time,
building up, running over the heather, speeding up the

hill and chasing among the trees. It had been waiting to burst its strength in the sudden wildness of a summer gale, coming from nowhere, lashing the trees in the forest, lashing the wild waves on the sea loch, till the deep blue was patched with a smother of white, and foam fled across the rolling water.

The boys ran and the flames followed them.

The forester looked up, saw the fire, cursed and raced to the telephone. He called for the fire engines, and warned those who lived among the trees that there was danger. The houseowners were driving out of the forest even before the boys reached the fire post, and the distant siren sounded on the air.

They could not warn the beasts that hid among the tall trees.

Fire!

Terror tang and rank reek. The squirrel had known fire before, had seen his mother die in the flames. He fled down the hillside, caring for nothing but to escape before the blaze reached him, taking his family with him, his mate and the two young. Their urgent paws sped over the pine needles, running away from the wind and the fear, running towards the water, running towards the bare beach where the sea soaked the weed and nothing could burn.

Time was so short.

The wind was rioting in the bushes, flinging long streamers of blazing light ahead of it, thrusting merry fingers into every bush and tree. It sped the terror before it, blowing and gusting, so that yellow fire swept along dry branches, red sparks dived from bush to bush and danced on the air, a fountain of colour, alive and hotter than horror.

The stags on the mountain lifted their heads, and the pinpoint fire below reflected in their glowing eyes. They turned to run.

Crash through the heather, speeding hooves over the mosses, plunging through the peat hags, bounding over the rocks—a mass of frightened bodies thundering away from the blaze, in a panic driven pack.

Halfway down the hill the hind herd joined them, body pressing against body, eyes wild and ears flattened, white scuts warning as they bounded. The calves followed, close against their mothers, some so young it was hard to keep up.

On, speeding down the mountain. On, driven by the need for safety. On, not hearing the scream of the engines, not heeding the men who ran with brushwood brooms and axes, and felled the bushes in the hope that the fire would not leap the barrier. The men beat at the flames that darted towards them, seeking to smother the onrushing fires before they became too great.

High on the hill the wildcat heard the noise of burning; she knew the terror roar that raged in the trees and brought her kittens, running, racing, clambering over rocks, not down to the fire, but above it, climbing, climbing, while the little ones sped after her, striving to keep up with her. Every now and then she stopped and carried one, desperate to put distance between herself and the devouring monster that ravaged on the hillside.

She was the first to find safety, high on the peak, almost in the eagle's nest, under a ledge where water dripped and where the four kittens stopped to lap, and where she lay and guarded them lest they fall, or the eagle see them. She stretched and watched the hillside turn from green to gold and yellow and scarlet, to darkling smoke and bitter, choking reek. She could not find a clear space in which to breathe, and their eyes stung and the air was foul.

Then the wind took pity and turned away, and the air cleared around them. Smoke poured over the fire fighters, down towards the stampeding stags, among the squirrels and over the loch.

Fear. And the mountain hare was among the stags, racing among the hooves. He was kicked and beaten and bruised as he sought a way through, a way that would lead from the encroaching flames, and take him to safety. Bound and leap and bound again, with flopping ears and startled tail, with the tease and choke of smoke in his throat, and the vision in front of him of the empty beach and the rolling water and the sanctuary away from the trees.

There were birds among the trees. Birds that flew with blazing feathers and plunged themselves in the tarns and streams where they could, knowing that water was their only hope. Birds that died as they fled. An owl that soared upwards, higher and higher above the forest, turned to the south away from the wind, and found his way to a distant moor. He cowered all night in a thorn tree and listened to the screams that sounded on the wind, and the roar, thunder, crackle and rage of the tearing fire.

Fire!

There were two otters in a holt on the hill. They stayed half the night in water, surfacing only to breathe, hidden

and secret, and surrounded by smoke that almost choked them. But for them too came relief when the wind changed and they survived.

Fire!

Mice scurried into deep holes, but holes were not safe for burning leaves could fall and catch the grass, and many were suffocated. A mole burrowed deep and ever deeper, for the ground above him was hot.

The foxes went to earth with the badgers, deep underground in chambers dug long ago for other reasons. Fire could not come here, but some passages were sour with smoke, and the beasts within them had to find others beds on which to lie lest they choke and die. One vixen, young and not yet wise, took her cubs and ran with the stags. One cub was so severely kicked that he limped for months, and his mother and brothers had to bring him food.

Down the long hillside, with the fire chasing them, with flames leaping from tree to tree, from branch to branch, with the wind speeding and spreading and mocking man's small efforts. Down, away from the tremendous passion born from a tiny seed, from one small match, from a little heap of shavings, fanned by the shouting gale that hurled a tree from the ground, as its roots lay shallow. The tree crashed and within moments was a mass of glowing red, a heap of ash, a memory only. The wind flicked along its trunk and the small sparks drifted along the ground, and rose in columns as they reached yet another tree, yet another bush.

The eagles flew to another peak and rested, and watched the flames eat everything they had known. They watched the packed brown backs of the running stags and saw the darting hare, and spied the vixen, but fear held them captive and the beasts ran untroubled and no creature thought of food.

The little roebuck and his doe and twin kids flitted downwards, slipping among the tree trunks, the smoke driving them to distraction.

The herons left the heronry and flew south, and stood along the pebbled beach watching the trees, which they had known for centuries, crash to the ground and vanish in the holocaust.

Fire!

Smoke blackened the sky and darkness came early. The hillside crackled with the roar of flames, the crash of dying

trees and the packed thunder of massing hooves. Down
through the mossy rides leaping the rocks, shouldering
aside companions, eyes only on the clean wide beach and
the raging sea that was now whipped by the wind to a
frenzy so that waves shocked the shore as they broke and
the foam scattered.

Noise was panic. Noise was terror. Noise was fear. Men
shouted to one another as they worked, cutting the undergrowth, felling the trees, widening the fire rides, trying
to contain the damage. In the fire station four boys sat
and watched, appalled by the destruction they had caused
in all innocence.

A gun sounded, and a flying bird dropped dead in a

blaze of feathers. There were more guns on the hill. The boys dared not think of the animals trapped among the trees, of the smoke-filled burrows and the terrified wildlings. They had never imagined such horror.

'A dry summer and one small match!' the fire ranger said, coming into the room, taking a beef sandwich from a plate that one of the other men had made ready for him. He ate swiftly and drank, and was away again, without a word to the boys, who had looked silently at his blackened face and scorched hands, and found themselves without words.

Never light fires under trees.

If only they had listened, but now it was too late.

The tide was rolling in from the sea, and the beach was narrowing fast. Animals packed at the edge of the water retreated before the tide, except for two stags who swam with the waves and reached a small island where they crawled, exhausted and battered, and stayed for the rest of the summer and only swam to the mainland again when the need for the hinds took them.

The otters swam downstream and found themselves a new home, away from the forest. They did not play that night. Fear had exhausted them and, when they were sure they were safe, they curled together, pressed close for company, and slept. Soon the female would be old enough for young. As yet she was too small.

When morning came the fire was only a grumble, a rumour in the sky, a trampled mass of blackened smoking earth, a deadening of trees from brittle branches that had lost their leaves, but not suffered more than scorching. The weary men continued to work, soaking the earth, beating down the sparks, watching till danger was past. No one had slept.

When the sun shone on devastation and the smoke was only a thin haze of cloud above the desolate forest, the fire ranger took the boys to the edge of the trees. They looked down on the packed beach where weary beasts lay side by side, red stag and hind and calf, roe deer and their kids, a fallow deer by itself in one corner, its antlers breaking the skin, the vixen with her cubs and the crouched hare.

The wind was gone. It whispered along the ground and brushed the blue silk of the waves and feathered them gently with foam. It stroked the fur of the crowded beasts, it seethed gently in the bushes.

The fire was dead.

The trees were dead.

The ground was dead.

The ranger drove the boys through the forest, saying nothing. There was no need for words. Davie had a burn on his hand and Roger had been struck by a burning branch across the face. None of them would ever forget.

'You can go,' the ranger said, when they came to the edge of the town. He opened the door.

'Go?' The boys had expected punishment.

'You came to us and told us what you had done. And it was an accident,' the man answered. 'I don't think you need any other lesson.'

They climbed out and stood on the path and watched the ranger drive away.

There was nothing to say to him or each other. They parted, each walking to his own home, each with a memory he wished he could forget but that he knew would stay with him as long as he lived. The memory of the running beasts, terrified by the horror that had been unleashed by one small match on the lonely hill where they had always lived their quiet lives, untroubled by man, browsing under the friendly shade of growing trees.

It would be a long time before trees grew again on the mountain.

STAY ON

Here are details of other exciting TARGET titles. If you cannot obtain these books from your local bookshop, or newsagent, write to the address below listing the titles you would like and enclosing cheque or postal order—*not* currency—including 7p per book to cover packing and postage; 2–4 books, 5p per copy; 5–8 books, 4p per copy.

TARGET BOOKS,
Tandem Publishing Ltd.,
14 Gloucester Road,
London SW7 4RD

If you enjoyed this book and would like to have information sent you about other TARGET titles, write to the address below.

You will also receive:
A FREE TARGET BADGE!
Based on the TARGET BOOKS symbol—see front cover of this book—this attractive three-colour badge, pinned to your blazer-lapel or jumper, will excite the interest and comment of all your friends!

and you will be further entitled to:
FREE ENTRY INTO THE TARGET DRAW!
All you have to do is cut off the coupon beneath, write on it your name and address in *block capitals*, and pin it to your letter. Twice a year, in June, and December, coupons will be drawn 'from the hat' and the winner will receive a complete year's set of TARGET books.

Write to:

TARGET BOOKS,
Tandem Publishing Ltd.,
14, Gloucester Road,
London SW7 4RD

If you live in South Africa,
write to:

TARGET BOOKS,
Purnell & Sons,
505, C.N.A. Building,
110, Commissioner Street,
Johannesburg

If you live in New Zealand,
write to:
TARGET BOOKS
Whitcoulls Ltd.,
111, Cashel Street,
Christchurch

If you live in Australia,
write to:

TARGET BOOKS,
Rical Enterprises Pty. Ltd.,
Daking House,
11, Rawson Place,
Sydney, N.S. Wales 2000

————————cut here————————

Full name...

Address...

....

....

Age...

PLEASE ENCLOSE A SELF-ADDRESSED ENVELOPE WITH YOUR COUPON.